BLOOMLAND

BLOOMLAND

A NOVEL

JOHN ENGLEHARDT

DZANC
BOOKS

5220 Dexter Ann Arbor Rd.
Ann Arbor, MI 48103
www.dzancbooks.org

Library of Congress Cataloging-in-Publication Data

Names: Englehardt, John, 1987- author.
Title: Bloomland : a novel / John Englehardt.
Description: Ann Arbor, MI : Dzanc Books, [2019]
Identifiers: LCCN 2019013628 | ISBN 9781945814938
Classification: LCC PS3605.N458 B58 2019 | DDC 813/.6--dc23
LC record available at https://lccn.loc.gov/2019013628

"Be Okay, It Will Be Okay" was first published in *Moss*; "From the Void I Saw Your Face" was first published in *Vol.1 Brooklyn*.

First US edition: September 2019
Interior design by Michelle Dotter

Printed in the United States of America

10   9   8   7   6   5   4   3   2   1

CONTENTS

For Katharine

BE OKAY, IT WILL BE OKAY

ROSE

Six years before college, you are under a queen-sized mattress with your grandma and brother. A cold front has descended from the Rocky Mountains into the Plains of Arkansas, where you live in a house with no basement. Just minutes ago, you walked barefoot into the street and beheld a half-mile-wide funnel cloud cutting across the horizon, the strangest gray you've ever seen, a sort of whirling, irradiated charcoal. Grandma told you to put on shoes and get under the mattress, and now she is reciting the Lord's Prayer. You are listening to hectoring gusts of wind, pictures and pill bottles smashing against the wall. Even under the mattress, you can tell when you're beneath a giant shadow. Grandma says not to grab hold of the mattress if it slips away, but when the walls heave outward and the mattress ascends, you can't help but grab after it. You are airborne and tumbling, swapping backdrops. Earth. Sky. Earth. Sky. Earth. At some point, you see a brown trail of destruction wending across the green countryside.

Your body lands on dirt, but the wind skips and drags you across it until you hit a retaining wall, which is actually your neighbor's house that has been reduced to a slab of concrete. Your face hits it, fracturing your skull and breaking your nose, but you don't feel that yet. You stand up. It's quiet, the sky a floating junkyard. A banker's chair. Chimney bricks. Hundred-pound manhole. Full-bloomed poplar tree. A garage door spinning like a frisbee into the distance.

You don't know where to stand, but that's irrelevant because the wind is pushing you. Your heels dig into the ground. Sideways debris stabs into your skin like candles into a birthday cake.

When it stops, sirens blare in the distance. RVs from the dealership down the road lie in ditches, shredded like paper. Amidst the ruin you find your grandmother, who at first is just a wad of disorderly gray hair, her body half-covered by a sheet of particleboard. You pull her out and dust her off, but she doesn't respond to your touch. Eventually, you scan the landscape for your brother, slowly realizing how lucky you were to find anything at all in this mosaic of rubble.

Your mom, who was shuffling cards at the casino in Alla Vista when the tornado hit, shows up in her truck, and she drives you to a medical triage outside the Dollar General where they poorly sew up the gash on your forehead and take all the debris out of your back. One thing they find is a metal pin engraved with the words MEL'S LOGGING COMPANY—IN GOD WE TRUST, which will be attached to your backpack when I meet you for the first time, many years from now.

Your mother takes you to live at her boyfriend's house, and over the course of the next year, she locks herself in the bathroom more and more. She treats you like a hole in the floor she has learned to avoid. She is harnessed to the couch with cheap rum, watching movies like *Home for the Holidays* in mid-July. Her boyfriend is a forklift operator who sleeps on a water bed and obsessively collects bottle caps, supposedly for some kind of "art project." He watches you sweep the kitchen like there's something inside you he's about to disinter. Then one day, he disappears, and your mom is alone in his room, yelling at a part of herself who cannot hear, surrounded by dirty clothes and cat litter ground into the carpet.

During this time, one of your teachers learns that you're stealing rolls of toilet paper from school to take home, and then CPS gets involved. Then it's foster homes. Edges of familial units. High school vicissitudes until finally you get adoptive parents. You change your name to Rose, work at the Baskin Robbins in the mall, use your 4-H leadership experience to qualify for a poultry science scholarship at Ozarka University, a flagship state school tucked away against one of the oldest mountain ranges in North America, where there never has been an F5 tornado, as far as you know.

When you visit, it's a land of white mansions on the edge of campus, yellow trumpets of daffodils, gigantic porch settees, and blonde girls walking in groups, all wearing the same high-waisted jean shorts. When you see how they study under dim chandeliers and cheer for the Ozarka Raccoon football team, you decide you want to join a sorority. Your adoptive parents advise against it, but you've been saving money scooping ice cream. You have enough to pay for annual dues.

Fall arrives, and you rush. You buy the right clothes. Force-smile so much that your face hurts. You line up and get honked at by every Jeep and scooter-driving male in the vicinity. You get into one of the most prestigious sororities, Beta Omega Kappa. The truth is, they think you're pretty—someone even says that scar on your forehead is charming, that it rips apart the conventionality of a pretty face. And you're calculating. You bury your accent, say "that would be lovely" like it's a catchphrase. You explain that you're originally from Alaska (though your only connection to that place is your biological father, who spent two summers there on fishing boats). You deflect unwanted attention by interrogating others. You learn to act like you're at the center of a small universe to which everyone else belongs.

So you stand there on the immaculate lawn with your sisters, in matching white mini dresses, two days before school starts, and they are teaching you the BOK cheer, which has a refrain that goes like this: "Be okay, it will be okay!" Amidst the high-spirited unison, you remember that all your life, you wanted to be this brand of normal—carefree, upper class, and virtuous by means of your inaccessibility—but you couldn't be. You imagined this normalcy as down some declivity in your heart, something you always had but could never reach. It was like growing up with an ocean outside of your bedroom window that disappeared when you looked at it. But now, on the BOK lawn, you feel like you are wading into its waters for the first time, and you are finding it is warm, and the sand is fine.

At first, you are overwhelmed by the frenetic 450-acre campus. There are tanning wipes and condoms in vending machines. Pasta bars. Students conducting Bible study in coffee shops, reading verse from iPhones, holding hands to pray while their legs squirm beneath tables. Hours' worth of coiffed hair. Lurid binge drinking. And when you go to see your advisor in the Don Butler Center for Poultry Excellence building, you walk past an eight-foot bronze statue of a rooster, wearing what looks like a crown of thorns on its head. Everything is hallowed. Everyone wants to know your name.

But when classes start, you find that all your professors are burned out teaching assistants who give you worksheets, overuse Powerpoint, speak in fake-authoritarian voices, or otherwise solicit class participation like manic-depressive game show hosts. Students shop for portable hammocks and watch cooking shows on their phones during lecture. Sometimes, you feel as if you're learning what you studied in high school, just in bigger rooms with nicer computers.

One of these classes is Eddie Bishop's section of English 120. His teaching style is one of controlled outrage, directed at everything except the students sitting before him, whom he attempts to "level with." When his class ends, you walk out of Campbell Hall onto the cobbled road. It's late in the day, so campus no longer looks like a bad TV show. There are no boys shouting from luxury SUVs. There are no officious "Help a Raccoon" stations, no high-fives, no slow-walking athletes, no student-ministers standing on five-gallon buckets, duct tape over mouths, holding signs that say I WILL NOT

BE SILENT ABOUT MY FAITH. No. It's just you under the sunset's dying lushness, the brutalist stone buildings. On these evenings, Eddie's lectures sometimes give you an emptied-out feeling, like you are un-learning the things you thought you knew. You decide that this is what you were looking for when you came to a university.

One day, Eddie makes everyone read a short story about a girl with a wooden leg who decides to be ugly. She changes her name to Hulga, studies philosophy, wears skirts with horses on them. Eddie says she wants ugliness to create a new self. She succeeds until a Bible salesman tricks her and steals her fake leg. You read a paragraph aloud in class—the one with her stranded and one-legged in a barn—then you raise your hand and say that the ugly girl no longer clings to her ugliness, she's just sad. Eddie nods. "We have to consider," he says, now pacing past the empty first row, "that our personalities are deep wells into which the world will drop ideas, desires, even other people. So, you have to be careful. You have to know what was down there in the first place."

This is when you begin to fear the thing you made inside yourself. You spend as much time on schoolwork as you do making posters with glitter glue. You always need a date. You've been tanning, and the fair-skinned girls are starting to ask if you're "mixed with something" (as in Mexican, though they often guess Italian). At parties, older boys hand you drinks they made in other rooms. They take you out onto sleeping porches and tell you not to be so stingy with your body. It all feels like the story about the ugly girl, except reversed.

All of this does not completely metastasize until a representative from Slendertone Fitness comes to the sorority. She has bins filled with bands that fit around your stomach and legs, sending shocks to your muscles to tone them. All the sisters who are infinitesimally "overweight" are named, encouraged to buy, and they do. You're not one of the "fat" ones, but after this encounter, you feel that your routine of long jogs and avoiding Chicken Finger Fridays wasn't for yourself after all, but was actually in preparation for this moment. Nowadays, even the things you thought you did for yourself were not. They were for the normal person you were creating, who is now metamorphosing within you.

Amidst all this, you think increasingly about your family. Some memories emerge so clearly from those hardscrabble days that you experience them again, as if for the first time. At twelve years old, you are with your mother at the mall, and you are watching her talk to the boy selling phones at the Verizon kiosk. Your mother asks for the cheapest one, fumbling with her welfare card, and the tattooed, multi-earringed boy grabs a clamshell phone from the case, price-matches it to another store, and gives it to your mother for free. On the way home, you consider the dirty summer dress your mother is wearing—the blue one swimming with cartoon fishes—and your own decaying shoes and barely healed forehead, and you decide you look like someone who needs to be given things.

You spend so much time evaluating boys the same age your brother would be that you become a connoisseur. Their posture, hair thickness, the shoulder from which their backpack hangs. One afternoon, you see a skinny, dark-haired boy in the park, eating a torta from La Super Quesadilla, his green flannel tucked into jeans, how the bright sun makes the grass around him look blanched. Is that him, staring ambiguously past the swings in your direction?

That night, you lie awake in your dorm with your laptop, studying your old neighborhood with Google Street View, and you find that the cameras haven't been back since the tornado hit. You click past your grandmother's house, the waist-high chain-link fence before the unkempt grass, sagging gutters, and chewed-up screen door. You click on the arrows until you're down at the Supermercado you used to walk to with your brother, and when you see two figures with garbled faces waiting at a crosswalk, sodas in hand, you cry so hard you can feel it deep in your jaw.

Lately, you've been feeling best when working on your term paper for Eddie's class. You've decided to write about the ugly girl, about the artificial things we lean on, like beauty and religion. You read Malebranche, study nihilism, meet with Eddie one on one in places like Starbucks and Slim Chickens because he doesn't like his office. He says things like "good stories have no meaning" and "you have to consider education as artifice." It all feels a little absurd, but at least it's an absurdity you're free to imitate. When you hand in the paper on the last day of class, all you can think about is getting it back. You will sit beside Eddie at a small coffee table, wearing a dress that you hope makes you look professional, all of your papers neatly aligned in a binder. At some point, his admiration will overflow, and he'll say something off-kilter, something like, "You have no idea who you are," but he will say it like a compliment. He will use words like incomparable, exacting, perigee. You will walk with him across the anodyne campus and into the afterlife of the person you once were.

This is what happens instead. A student walks into the library during finals week with a modified Chinese-type SKS assault rifle, then opens fire, killing eleven students and an instructor. All campus activities are suspended for a week, and during this time you hear a rumor that he left behind a video the FBI will not release. Barbara Walters comes out of retirement to interview the father of the shooter on primetime television. News teams book every hotel room in the city limits, and everyone keeps saying "tragedy" with vague disdain, as if the shooting was just a mad dream, not some kid adding his personal darkness to a collective shadow that had already spread across our lives. Still, at night, when you overhear prayers through the vents, you clasp your hands and listen. You sleep with the blinds closed and the fluorescent lights on.

When the university publishes a list of the victims, you find out that one of them is Casey Bishop—Eddie's wife. You go online to confirm this, and find a picture of three people on a hiking trip, standing with their backs turned to a bluffline somewhere in the Ozarks. One of them is unmistakably Eddie, with his precise beard and thin, flyaway hair. The other two people you don't know. Me, with an overblown smirk, the kind that now belongs to an abandoned version of myself. And Casey, wearing a billowy sweater, bangs cutting across her eyes. She's baring her teeth like she is half smiling, half preparing to battle the stranger we asked to take the photo. You look too long and she becomes fixed, the way dead people become their own archetypes, how they take you back to the honeysuckle and azaleas and lichen-covered rocks and rolling hills that surrounded them. Back there, time is so habitable. It is infinite.

On the day campus reopens, you want to walk to the English department to see if your paper will be there, wondering if Eddie graded them before all this happened. But you're afraid of campus— everyone is. Eventually, you rationalize that this is probably the safest the campus will ever be, so you step onto the bright sidewalks, past a media cavalcade at the on-campus hotel, where news helicopters buzz overhead.

Your paper is in a box on the floor with sixty others. There are a few sentences underlined, and on the back page, scrawled in blue ink, Eddie has written THIS PAPER IS BEAUTIFUL. The irony of such a statement is not lost on you—it makes you think there is some critique embedded in it, like your paper is beautiful in the same way that the ugly girl is ugly.

So you walk back to your dorm, through a campus that has police officers leering down every corridor. It is winter now, and cresting one hill, you can see the far-reaching gray of leafless trees, undulating over hilltops and eventually into the delta—the cemeteries and chicken houses, the puddled roofs of Wal-Marts, Baptist churches with helicopter pads, and into the plains where you'll spend the next three months, over Christmas break. You planned to feel excited, incubated, to sleep like you're in a childhood room, to smile straight into the pageantry of university life. Instead, college feels like a roller coaster that disappeared before ascending its first peak, one that has left you staring down onto the world from a stranded place in the sky.

WHAT GOT YOU HERE WILL NOT GET YOU TO YOUR FUTURE

EDDIE

THE MOST UNFLAGGING WOMAN you will ever meet enters your life during sophomore year of college, the same time you stop believing in God. What this means is the zealotry that has been ingrained in you—the kind that has involved obsessing over sin and faith and the fact that Jesus should be the only fixed point of reference in the dark room of your life—can be directed at something else now. Her name is Casey. You are watching her square dance in a living room with all the furniture pushed against the walls, slowly realizing that you recognize her as the unabashed-pregnant-teenager character from a university theater production. This makes the disorganized grace of her dancing, her black wavy hair, and the cream-colored skirt she wears (that she will later describe as "kindergarten teacher chic") seem both familiar and new. When the dance ends, you follow her to the back porch, quietly preparing a compliment on her acting. Everyone is sweating, drinking wine from mason jars, looking past ancient stands of cypress trees and into the scattered stones of a confederate cemetery. Other than telling her your name is Eddie, you won't remember what exactly you say. But you will remember how unique this moment feels, like two swimmers from separate shores meeting in the open water. The two of you talk and promenade and swing your corners until the only people left at the party are the hosts and an irascible drunk who keeps asking to play the banjo. Then you walk her back to her apartment, where you talk until the sun comes up, hoping to obscure the fact that you are too nervous for falling asleep or going home or kissing—it is an anxiety that, as a well-adjusted adult, you will yearn for but not experience again.

The next day, you wake up to the sound of something gigantic coming at you. At first it is a faint, squabbling "whoop" sung by a chorus of ghosts, and then it gets louder, becoming a tornado of screams that you worry is the sound of your soul getting sucked out of the world and into a canyon of hell. But then the yells turn into a cheer: "Ozarka Raccoons, go!" You realize it is homecoming weekend. Casey is asleep on the carpet beside the couch. Soon you can hear music blaring from a fraternity down the street, which alternates between glossy Americana and dance club ass worship.

Casey wakes up. "We have to get out of here," she says.

In terms of identity, you are learning how easy it is to cross from one territory into another. Just last year, you would have gone to church on a day like this one, stood in a sea of khakis and listened to pastor Ronnie Boyd deliver a sermon titled "What Got You Here Will Not Get You To Your Future," which you will later classify as just another cryptic, pseudo-intellectual way to rant about sin and convince you to hate the choices you've made your entire life. Afterward, you would have changed out of your khakis into jeans and a Raccoon T-shirt, got drunk at a tailgate party, and evaluated sorority girls with that normalized tone of scorn/adoration. You even would have cheered when a Jeep drove by parading a flag with a crude drawing of a muscular raccoon sexually dominating University of Alabama's cartoon elephant, "Big Al."

But instead you are waking up late, hungover and un-showered. You are riding in the passenger seat with a girl singing along to The Velvet Underground, a girl who keeps bones of dead animals on the dashboard for good luck. At the edge of town, the smell in the air shifts from barbecue sauce to chicken shit. Casey drives past fields of yellow flowers, hot armadillo carcasses, feedmills, burnt mansions, onto dirt roads and over rainwater streambeds. She says she wants to stop by her parents' property, an organic farm that sounds quaint until you arrive at a wood-paneled double-wide beyond which wild packs of dogs lurk, waiting to take down cattle, and into her parents' living room/dining room/kitchen, where she is rummaging through drawers looking for their stash of pot.

After you smoke a bowl, Casey takes you to a drive-in at the edge of the shuttered town square. She buys fried pickles and butterscotch shakes, then parks her car on the top of Pension Mountain. Out here, airplane navigation lights lacerate the sky, and she tells you about the owner of Butler Chicken Company, who apparently has a private airport he only uses at sundown.

"Human trafficking?" you ask.

"Definitely," she says. "But you should be careful with that term. It has been co-opted by people who oppose sex workers in general. You could give me a pickle for a blow job and be arrested for human trafficking."

"I had no idea," you say, no longer comfortable holding the pickles in your lap. You set them on the dash, stare out into the reddening clouds. At this point, you convince yourself that you might love Casey, though years later, you will look back on this moment and regret how obvious and shallow you were, how the manic beauty you admired in her was just an attempt to possess what you viewed to be your opposite. How labeling her a quirky girl meant you didn't have to take her seriously.

"Do you think I talk too much?" she says after a long silence, with an edge of hostility.

"Absolutely not," you respond. And right now, you mean it. She is speaking to you like she just got rescued from a deserted island, like she's never really been able to share her life with someone, and here you are—finally. And as the flushed hills of autumn peel away into a sunset that's still wavy with heat, you feel as if your heart will never vacillate again.

In those early days, sometimes you still reach after the disappearing beacon of God. You pray the sinner's prayer in your sleep. You take long showers after sex, your still-tumescent cock throbbing with guilt. Then you get comfortable enough around Casey to redirect your psychic energy, and instead of brooding over things like The Doctrine of Total Depravity, you put your energy into loving and supporting another person. When Casey decides to cut her hair short, you do it for her. You buy her presents. You edit her English papers. You say, "I don't care if you don't shave your armpits." She says, "Your cum is translucent, like I'm looking at the moon." When you tell her about the recurring nightmare you have of your father shouting, "Are you or are you not on fire for God, faggot?" she says that's awful, and you are not a freak, and it is normal—considering all you have been through. Then, at a certain point, you realize how completely you have turned your back on Jesus Christ, replacing him with a girl. You don't care. The de-numbed and elated mood you're in with Casey feels like it has been with you all your life. It takes no effort to believe it exists.

Over the course of the next two years, this is how you know your love is sustainable. You will be walking to your poetry seminar and you'll see Casey alone, through the large magnolia trees that look like freeze-frame explosions, and she will look sad. You will watch from the audience as she plays a partly crippled mental patient in a Sam Shepard play. You will listen as she talks to her sister, and they will laugh at the same time, in the exact same way. These moments give you a seeing-your-elementary-school-teacher-in-the-supermarket feeling. You can't believe she's real. Especially not outside the context of your relationship. It will make you think how many aspects of this person are, at this point in your relationship, impossible for you to know. That is love, you think—that's it.

So you get married, and not because it's financially practical (it's not) or because your parents want it (fuck them) or even because it feels right (it doesn't), but because your feelings are so strong that they scare you. They need to be contained somehow. I still think about you two every time one of my students gets engaged. The cynic in me is honestly happy for them, as I would have been for you, because in the end, what better or worse chance did you and Casey have than the rest of us?

The year before you graduate college, before both of you get rejected by every masters program except the one at Ozarka, you move in together. You live in a small stone house at the edge of campus. One with a metal roof and a basement inhabited by camel crickets. Not much seems to change, except you hang around when Casey has incapacitating migraines, and you find it funny when she smears Bengay all over her face until it is numb. You pick up her prescriptions at the Wal-Mart on campus. You carry her around the house after she breaks her leg painting Juliet's balcony at the theater and exhaust "break a leg" jokes until she starts slapping you. But you have a few worries. For example, the worry that you and Casey are actually too supportive, and that this supportiveness fosters a kind of instant gratification dynamic, so that the moment you feel a thing you are done feeling it. Or the worry that the same thing is happening with love that it did with God, and at some point you will be standing there, saying to yourself, "Believe in Love. Believe in Love *now!*" and it will not work. Or the worry that Casey is the only woman you've ever had sex with, and that you lost your virginity to her and cried into a pillow without her noticing (because what a stupid thing to cry about) was the first misstep in a long series of emotionally cagey actions that are hiding some kind of True Weakness. But these worries are so faint that they are either completely imagined, or they are so deep-rooted that they can't be seen from the surface. They might, you admit to yourself, be worries that turn into actual problems down the road, but you are still so young and so near the beginning of the relationship that imagining your future is like thinking of what the Earth will look like when the Sun burns out.

NO FEAR

ELI

WHEN THE MEDIA LOOKS BACK on your life, they will point to one night in particular that supposedly begins your transition from a "normal" kid to a pathological young man bound for large-scale violence, and it starts at Alfredo Café in Earl Heights. Your mother waits tables here, and she is getting cut from her section two hours early. It's been a slow night. Her last table wrote on the check, "I already give God 10 percent, why should you get 15?" She is folding napkins with Amy, a coworker who usually spends her shift talking about celebrity crushes. Amy asks your mom out for a drink. She knows the band playing at Stroman's tonight. She has a cute shirt your mom can change into. She'll drive.

In the low-lit employee bathroom, Amy's tank top sucks in your mom's stomach and exaggerates the squareness of her shoulders. While twisting in the cloudy mirror, she tries to imagine getting buzzed from a few drinks, then coming home to your half-awake father in this shirt. This is important because, recently, your mom has needed to imagine she is having sex with your father in order to come, which includes the moments she's actually having sex with him. Even on top, looking down, she has to re-imagine some earlier time, when it was somehow better, even though it's the same person she's seeing, from the same angle. She's worried that she can only be attracted to your father's avatar. Alcohol usually helps.

The guy Amy knows is Joe Graves, a one-man-band who plays frantic country-blues with a stomp box, banjo, harmonica, and a swift, nasally voice that captures the room's attention like shattering glass. He has red suspenders and a pointy beard. Amy is clearly taken by him, as she's on her third vodka tonic by the time Joe's set ends, and is in that drunken state where she feels her body is some courageous puppet of her thoughts. Amy keeps saying, "Should I talk to him?" And your mother responds, "Yeah don't you know him?" But Amy is not listening. She is taking the hairband from her wrist and fastening her hair into a bun. She is following Joe into the smoker's pit outside.

It's the only bar in this part of town that doesn't allow smoking inside, and the smoker's pit is just a large cage made with chicken wire and plywood. Your mom is leaning against the wire, the pattern digging into her shoulders, when a young man wearing a tie starts talking to her. He gives her a business card, which has DJ TODD and VOICE TALENT printed at the bottom. It's that time of the night when everyone has new drinks but no one remembers buying them.

Then your mom is in Amy's car, a 1987 Toyota hatchback that looks like a giant roller skate. They are on a county road. Oncoming vehicles are flicking their brights on and off with measured confidence. Your mom is speeding through the galaxy of variables that many media reporters, nine years later, will latch onto, saying that what is about to happen is the main reason you did the thing that no one can understand. You did not emerge from the sanctity of a normal nuclear family—that's what they will find most reassuring.

The first officer on the scene finds Amy's car wedged beneath the rear of a parked tractor-trailer, like a doorstop. The driver's seat is empty. The roof is peeled off the top of the car, and something like steam is coming out of the fully reclined passenger seat. Moving forward, when he has the angle to look down into the vehicle, he finds a body so crushed it looks inside out, uncreated. He realizes that the steam is actually coming from the still-warm insides of your mother, and for a moment he watches as it floats away and blends into the early morning fog, past the bare trees and into the expressionless sky.

You actually don't remember the next week of your life. The darkness defends it from your knowing. Within this darkness, you attend your mother's funeral. Amy is put in an emergency psychiatric facility for a month (they found her in the woods after the crash with only a few scratches, on the phone with her parents). Your father files a wrongful death suit against her, seeking $600,000 in damages. The suit gets dismissed.

The first time you cry, or remember crying, is two weeks later, when you overhear your father on the phone. He says, "A son losing his mother is the single most traumatic thing that can happen to a boy Eli's age." And the fact that you cry instantaneously makes you think there is something wrong with the way you grieve. It makes you think that you can't actually be sad unless someone else spells it out for you.

In the year that follows, a therapist named Anne instructs you to play with puppets and draw scenes of your life with colored pencils. But you don't feel like you're meeting with someone. You feel like you're in a waiting room, losing yourself in the dusty speckled carpet. Eventually, Anne diagnoses you with something called "adjustment disorder," which your father refers to as a "bogus condition" since its only treatment is more therapy, something he can no longer afford.

You and your father become coequals in desperation. He brings you into the living room and calls your mom's cell on speakerphone so the two of you can hear her voice. He tells you she sang "Moon River" in the shower. She wanted to teach you violin. She had this way of helping people find themselves through her. But eventually, the result is that his image of her becomes superimposed over your own memories. Your mother becomes like a moment you only re-member because a photograph of it exists. So when your father wants to talk, you start hiding. You lock yourself in the bathroom with magazines and bowls of cereal. You lie on the plush bathroom rug and look up at the bluish light coming through the frosted window, pretending you're part of a sci-fi experiment. You're in a pod that has been shot into outer space. Your father kicks in the door once, only to realize you're not hurting anyone, being in there. He leaves you alone after that, starts shitting in the yard behind the shed. You stay in the bathroom for five hours. For ten. For seventeen. He just wants you to be close and safe, but years later, he will wonder if this taught you to value control, secrecy, and disconnection, that love compensates for nothing. He will picture all those hours you spent alone, scanning the room with no object in mind, finding fleeting splotches in your peripheral vision—a crow, a beetle—and worry that you were actually going somewhere very far away.

But your life is not without moments of levity. Like when your dad walks into your room while you are playing *NFL Blitz* or *Downtown Reconnaissance* on your Playstation and asks beseechingly if he can join, before grabbing a controller. Or that time he builds two canoes—one for each of you—as a Christmas present. He asks you what colors and what tagline you want stenciled to the side of the boat. You say black and red, and that the tagline should be NO FEAR. His is green and yellow, and it says GONE FISHIN'. You will spend a litany of mornings on that boat, paddling with ease on the placid water of Horseshoe Lake, and you will regard the early morning fog without a sense of awe or horror, because no one dared to tell you that detail of your mother's accident, thank god.

One story that will later emerge from your early teenage years, that will appear in a redacted journal the *Arkansas Post* will publish, is how the family that lives in the trailer park down the road has a strange revolving door of animals. Pygmy goats, llamas, giant rabbits, chow chows. The animals just appear, wander haplessly around their yard for a month, then vanish. You ask your father if they breed animals, and he shrugs his shoulders. Then one day you find a mewling, grey-bearded Labrador down by the river. You bring her home, name her Dusty. Your father instructs you to take her over to the family to see if she's theirs, and so you knock on their door and say, "Is this your dog?" They let Dusty in and say, "Thanks." You say, "No, is this your dog?" They say "Thanks" again. They shut the door in your face. For the next month, you watch the dog take her last wanderings around the property, until she eventually disappears like the rest.

When it's clear that Dusty is gone forever, you decide to approach your father, hoping he will find some container for your loss. He is sitting in his armchair, watching baseball highlights on his laptop. As you mope toward him, dragging your feet on the thick carpet fiber, he does not change his position. He turns toward you with an increasingly familiar stare, free of malevolence, but nevertheless communicating that you are not to be acting this way.

So you say nothing, go back to your room, where rage presents itself as the easy way back to feeling. In your journal, you fantasize about murdering the family in order to save the dog, concluding with the line, "Sometimes hate is the only thing I can love." The newspapers will have a field day with that one.

You get older, but you wonder if you're failing to incorporate your mother's death into your understanding of the world, if your unspoken grief will always be a fulcrum of your identity. For example, the main joy you get from succeeding in school or making friends is that the world will be that much sadder when you leave it. So, when a History teacher gives you a "C" on a term paper about Social Darwinism, you consider suicide. When a girl you met in a summer camp for culturally and economically deprived teens breaks up with you, you consider suicide. And when a gang of stray cats eats a bucket of Kentucky Fried Chicken you and a friend bought with your own money and left out on the porch, you consider suicide. The adults around you notice that you are mechanizing yourself against loss, that you still hide in the bathroom when guests come over, but they know there is no place in the world for a sad young man, so instead of engaging this behavior, they pathologize it. They wonder openly why you are so sensitive, so easily bruised, such a fool.

Then in eleventh grade, you get Mr. Madsen for American Literature. He is five feet tall, wears a jet-black toupee that looks like an ill-fitting helmet, and is the self-proclaimed largest collector of Billy Corgan paraphernalia. His teaching style is discursive chaos, and when too many students speak at once he often shakes his fists and yell-whispers, "Despite all my rage, I am still just a rat in a cage!" He cares very little about grades and assignments, and for the first time in your life, you're reading. You feel it sets you apart from your intolerantly holier-than-thou, ultra-Christian peers, who are so obtuse they read an entire novel without realizing the narrator got his dick shot off in World War I.

It is in this class that you write your first short story, "The Tortoise Woman," which depicts a thinly-veiled-version-of-yourself narrator who follows around an unpopular fat girl. He spends most of the story explaining in tactless, florid language how fat she is. Then he basically wonders aloud if she is even human. "Look at her," he says, "does anyone love her?" At the end of the story, he devises a plan to eat so much that he becomes a "tortoise man," so both characters have someone to love and understand. But he can't get fat. He eats everything, and nothing changes. "I can't even succeed at being a loser," he laments. Then he shoots himself.

Not surprisingly, this story lands you a private meeting with Mr. Madsen. He begins by explaining how stories are difficult to write, because the author often starts with a shallow misunderstanding of his own characters. This, of course, is teacher-speak for "Your writing is ignorant and shameful." But you don't interpret it that way. After all, "alarming" is what you were going for. Madsen pats you on the back, says he's required to send you to the school counselor.

The counselor wears plaid pants and has posters of both Shakespeare and Dr. Dre on her wall. All she does is ask questions about your home environment, because at this point in your life, your identity stretches across the thresholds of grief, puberty, and miseducation. To her, you are not innately broken, you're just another teenage boy who, through art, is learning to indulge in violent fantasies, who has already decided there is no hope for a lost soul trying to reconnect.

And yet, by the time you graduate high school, you think you are happy. You've transitioned from a social nonentity to a token bookworm, which means you've learned to view education as a mark of your superiority. When you study, you are outside the life of emotion. And when you return, you lament how ignorant people are, staring into the ghostly lights of cell phones. You, on the other hand, are a writer now. You read *Candide* by Voltaire. You talk to Mr. Madsen on his cell phone about college applications. Your father loosens up, starts offering guidance. He says cardiovascular exercise is more effective than psychological debriefing. He says if you act fragile then other people will treat you as if you are fragile, and you'll be cut off from the truth. He buys you a ten-year-old BMW, presumably to help your social status (which it does, a little bit). And then in August you drive across the state, past the decrepit barns, cow pastures, the rural Wal-Marts and billboards that say ANTI-RACISM IS ANTI-WHITE, and into the red hills of Ozarka University. On some days, you relish this journey like some beat generation writer, always on the move. This is how you erase your grief, by not looking back. Your happiness feels epiphanic. Your depression had been like having your hand stuck inside the malicious-looking jaw of a taxidermied animal, one that, for your entire life, you thought was real.

So when you arrive at Ozarka University for the first semester of college, you are as comfortable as you ever have been. Sure, you don't have many friends, and you don't have much success talking to girls, but that feels typical. You wear flip-flops and basketball shorts, walk to the dining hall with your student ID on a lanyard around your neck. You write excessively lyric composition papers lamenting our overblown PC culture. You tell your roommate that the girls in your dorm would be cute if they "just went to the gym." You skip several hours of student orientation to organize your room, which includes positioning your folded underwear in a drawer so that they will rotate evenly. You listen to "More than Words" by Extreme on repeat. You write the lyrics on the whiteboard above your desk. You are boring. And if there's any way I can avoid sounding like your apologist, it's to say the one thing that will enable your ambush is how deeply normal it is, this mask you've been taught to wear.

During this hiatus, time disobeys you less and less. It does not carry you back to when you were twelve years old, to a loss that is primitive and incontrovertible. It does not cause you to realize that your mother was the one who turned all the unused lights off, who filled the house with music. It doesn't make you cry and throw your backpack across rooms. And this is strange, because all your life you thought her death was the thing connecting and indebting you to the origin of your pain. But now it doesn't seem to matter. Your mother died in a car crash. Who cares? The accident by which people die is the same accident by which they live.

Yet you still have trouble speaking. At times it interferes with your desire to construct the normal male student identity you have imagined for yourself, but you've also learned that if you're quiet, people often just assume you're smart. They don't realize that some back part of your brain is cataloging what life owes to you, creating a deep well of perceived marginality. Besides, it just looks like you are squinting into a harsh light. Like you are nervous. Like there's a distracting jangle in your head. It is not obvious that you are a hook about to snag upon an ugliness out there in the world. That it's waiting for you.

Then one night, you exit the library into a crowd of students. All of them are pointing their phones at the sky. The entire horizon is green. Not like a sunset, but a deep, action green. It is below the blue and white twilight of stars and clouds. People are whispering. Toxic gas, chemical warfare, poison. They are running in the opposite direction. They are no longer reading *The Road to Reality* or writing personal reflection papers, or accusing a stranger of stealing their Northface jacket at the last house party. They are lost in the ethos of an emergency.

Hours later, the university will release a statement, saying the green haze was caused by facilities testing out the new thirteen-million-dollar big screen installed in the football stadium, that it has the kind of luminosity that can be seen from space, and green is the color it is when you turn it on. But for now, you are looking at the sky without fear. You regard it like a storm that loves you, feeling something deep within you beg for it. Then you go home and write about a voice you heard, and you say it's not really a voice, but more like an electrical current running through you. You write that you feel happy, that the voice allowed you to stand in wonder at a deep pain that would, for once, be shared. And it's this remark that will become one of the most misleading clues you leave behind. Because while this admission might point toward how small and degenerate your world has become, what people will latch onto is not what the voice says, but the fact that you heard one. It is this voice that made you evil and deranged, that will speak to you from an abstract hell conveniently placed outside our understanding. It is this voice, we will say, that tells you to kill.

FROM THE VOID I SAW YOUR FACE

EDDIE

SOMETHING IS WRONG WITH your marriage. What that thing is, you don't know. It can only be clarified by petty grievances. The actual problem must be some singular misunderstanding buried under an old road you've repaved. You can't navigate it because you don't know how it used to look.

For example, Casey has been leaving you at home while she goes to underground noise-metal shows with increasing regularity. There are three venues in town. One is called The Riot Room: an upstairs bar that features plastic chandeliers, a stage that also functions as a bathroom hallway, and warped wood floors with gaps so big that change falls through them. The other is a garage on MLK right behind the Cowboy Disco, which also serves as an artist studio/apartment. The third one is the house where Seth Avery lives. Seth is a roving bartender who wears cutoff jean shorts year round, decorates his living room with tinsel-framed cartoons, and often bites his guitar strings until he gets electrocuted.

Casey sees bands like Septic Vibes, Moon Machete, Nothingfriends. Their live shows are nightmarish construction sites of grinding feedback and sonorous, detuned drums. But this is how Casey likes it, when music is so loud it pushes her back against a wall, so she feels it in her chest more than she hears it. She says it's like meditation, when sound blocks out everything except itself. She goes to several shows a week, often coming back after last call and crawling into bed half drunk, smelling of body odor and cigarette smoke.

Years ago, you thought Casey's affinity for this music scene was a charming eccentricity. You went to a few of these shows and enjoyed the lack of posturing, expensive equipment, and delusions of grandeur. But now you feel out of place. You start wondering if the crowd is acting out an unfettered angst you've grown beyond. It makes you worry that, somewhere along the way, as you and Casey became different people, you didn't check that your new selves would be compatible.

You are not entirely aloof, so you mention this worry to Casey. You just want to talk, but what happens is both of you revert to your defensive behavioral patterns. "Why do you wait so long to address something that bothers you? Why don't you ever just get mad?" she says. "It's complicated," you say, "because I'm mad at myself for being mad at you." The two of you talk until you're too exhausted to disagree anymore, and things get better—until something else comes along. Your arguments have become so confined and circular that it feels like you're on the set of an absurdist family drama.

This is when you start spending most of your time at my house. You sit dejectedly on my enclosed porch, where the maple leaves gather in piles under dining chairs and recycling bins, turning pale and purple. It starts with a jacket you leave on my couch, then your running shoes. Soon it's your toothbrush and duffel bag. You sit on the washing machine wedged in my pantry as I cook dinner and you tell me how your marriage is wrecking the way a car crashes slowly, like when your father drove through a guardrail, then asked if everyone was okay while his truck was still tumbling down an embankment. We listen to pop ballads, read quotes from student papers. "Patriarchy treats women like escape goats." My recycling bin overflows with empties of cheap beer, and there are times when we silo ourselves so completely that we think being small-town professors has granted us entry into some high and mighty misunderstood club. We idealize being lost, and heartbroken, and overeducated, and in debt—but only because we have outrun the darkness that was coming for us, as if together we are moving toward some great yet colorless light.

Then one day, you wake up on my couch at six in the morning. You should be hungover, but you're completely awake. So you walk down the bike trail to The Depot, a train station built in 1901 that has been remodeled into a Chipotle Grill flanked by a coffee shop called Common Grounds. You get black coffee with cinnamon and grade papers on the cold back deck. An antique train lurches by, and from inside, the gray-haired tourists look upon you with empty surprise. Then in the distance, you are certain you see Casey walking to class alone. She is wearing her purple tights, the same ones a student insulted on her first-ever teacher evaluation. "Worst fashion sense *ever*!" the girl wrote under the question, "How would you rate your instructor's spoken English?" You think about how frequently Casey has worn those tights since then, how if someone doesn't like a part of who she is, she amplifies it. When she gets out of sight, you feel sick. You don't like the ease with which she just entered and left your day. You decide that rejecting her is like rejecting yourself—that the two of you have gone so far down a road together that no one else could possibly understand who you are.

So this is what you do. You invite yourself to the next show at The Riot Room. You start drinking early. You try standing patiently in the bathroom doorway while Casey winds a curling iron around her bangs, wearing black combat boots, black jeans, a leather coat, and red lipstick. But you're already battling an unresolved thread of frustration: she is dressing this way for a scene, and not to please you, and this confuses your screwed-up idea of what she owes you.

So as you walk downtown together, you ask about teaching, and she tells you how a student came into her office, said snow was a symbol for cold in Fitzgerald's "Winter Dreams," then ran away as if from a feral animal. In an attempt to be validating and encouraging, you tell her to keep in mind that these freshmen have it rough. That a lot of them barely escaped from towns where the main employers are Dollar General, Ciba Chemicals, and greasy diners that scrape up the high school dropouts and crackheads. Many of them are too afraid to drive "in the city," let alone talk to a young and incandescent professor.

"So, they're like me," says Casey, with an air of irritation.

"Yeah," you say, trying to backpedal. "Except no one is like you."

"Bullshit," she says.

The Riot Room is on the town square by the clock tower. It's wedged between a conservative used bookstore and a tanning salon. You can already hear the doomy guitars four blocks away.

Inside, a band called Brutal Push plays what sounds like a slow-motion funeral procession. Behind them hangs a homemade banner with a reanimated corpse baring sharp teeth, blood pouring from its mouth. You don't recognize anyone here, and the crowd is indifferent to your entrance, like a freeway swallowing you into its traffic. To the side of the stage, a woman dances by kicking her feet toward nothing.

So here it is, without warning—the problem that's like a cockroach scurrying beneath the stove whenever you step into the kitchen. Why would Casey ever choose this over you? It makes you want to go home, smoke a conservative amount of weed together, and wait for Casey to pull the anthology of haikus off the shelf like she used to. You want her lips to be provocative with surprise as she reads the words unnecessarily loud, the way she did when you were alone together. "A cloud floats/at the same place in the sky/where yesterday it floated." You want her to say, "I love you," in that small room where the air is bodyhot and tropical. But this is just a glossy reproduction of how things used to be. You're constantly re-learning that to dig up a memory with nostalgia is to erase it.

When the song ends, it's like a demented HVAC has been shut off, but then the lead singer fiddles with his effects pedals, the drummer slaps his sticks together, and it's on again. Drums emerge from dissonance. Yelling sprawls across overdriven bass. Casey pulls you closer to the stage, and you try to remember that the reason you came here was to show how solicitous you could be. But you realize what's scary about this place is not that she prefers it to you, but that there's a good reason why she likes it here. After all, she must also be worn down by sleeping with a passive-aggressive shoulder turned to you, masturbating alone in the shower, and constantly interpreting someone else's anxiety as a personal attack. She has to be bothered by the fact that your fights are like earthworms growing new heads after getting torn apart. And maybe she's closer to finding out why than you ever will be. Maybe she is not trying to sleep with Seth Avery or ignore you or drink until the world floats upon water. She is waiting in the wraith-like smoke for a deeper understanding that is separate from you. She wants to discern the exact reason why sound can carry so much that it becomes deafening, why love can mature into a void.

THE PROMISED LAND

ELI

ONE OF MANY TEACHERS WHO will later be attacked for overlooking your alarming disengagement is Dr. Fern, a psychology department head who brings a portable fan everywhere she goes. Due to a shortage of classrooms at the university, she teaches in a science lab. She lectures from behind a large counter lined with beakers and an industrial sink, sometimes washing her hands or fondling glassware in the silence of rhetorical questions. But most days she sits on a stool, legs crossed, gray hair whipping behind her like she's traveling forward into the rows of students. When she sits like this, you can almost picture her face before it was cluttered with experience. If you concentrate hard enough, she starts to look like your mother.

It is during these classes that you actually feel some curiosity suctioning at your heart. After all, you're into your second semester of college, and already it feels like some communal joke. Coming here was supposed to give you ideals to help navigate the seas of adulthood. It was supposed to provide a social milieu of comfort and friendship. You imagined it as some bloomland of romance and psychological growth. Instead, it has given you nights alone in a cinderblock dorm room. An English TA who made you write a cultural analysis of a Disney movie. A gym so crowded you ride the stationary bike in the corner like an old woman. Sometimes, you feel like you have retreated to a sliver of life that you can't even call your own.

Then you begin the unit on psychopathology, and Dr. Fern talks about substance-related disorders. At some point she asks everyone what causes drug addiction. Addictive personalities? Oral fixations? Chemical imbalances? She shrugs at the class. Consider two experiments, she says. In the first experiment, you put a rat alone in a cage with two water bottles. One bottle has regular H2O, and the other is laced with cocaine. Nearly every time you conduct this experiment, the rat becomes so obsessed with the cocaine that he drinks it until he dies. Drugs are addictive, right? Now consider the second experiment. You put several rats in a cage with the same water bottles, but it's not just a cage, it's a sort of rat city. There are colored balls, bowls of premium rat food, a maze of tunnels—you get the point. So, what happens in rat city? (Here she pauses for dramatic effect, picking up an Erlenmeyer flask to examine its emptiness). Nobody gets addicted, she says. Nobody dies. So maybe it's not about hedonistic partying or chemically hijacked brains. It's about isolation. It's about the life you have been given. Are you in a good cage, or a bad one?

This is the first time you consider that you are becoming a product of your seclusion. That, throughout your life, you have bonded with your isolation because you can't bond with anything else. And now, as a result, you've developed some kind of Stockholm syndrome with your depression. You have made it into a friend so you no longer have to perceive it as a weakness.

After class, you go to the small bathroom around the corner and begin taking a piss in the vintage urinal that looks like a giant mandible. A guy comes up beside you, spreading his legs wide and cracking his neck. He wears steel-toed boots, black socks, small shorts that expose his hairy thighs, and a tie-dye ball cap. You know his name is Gordon because he's one of the most outspoken students in Dr. Fern's class.

"Should have given them rats some fucking marijuana," he says.

"Why?"

He laughs. "You smoke weed? It's hard to tell, looking at you." Gordon sizes you up, but both of you are still pissing. Your instinct is to turn your shoulder, but then you'd be urinating into the corner.

The thing is, you're painfully aware that you don't look like anything in particular. You're not in a frat, not part of the rich kid ascendant order, though for the past year you've been trying to look like it. You cuff your khakis, tuck in your plaid shirts like some kind of mini-father. You drive an expensive car, listening to rap and country when it's about drugs, money, or women, but not when it's about tragedy or adversity. You've assimilated well enough that one night you followed a group of brothers through the back door of SAE and into a party. You didn't speak to anyone. You stole some punch that was spiked with cold medicine. You joined a group of guys who convinced a disoriented girl to climb onto the stripper pole mounted next to the DJ stage. Eventually, someone asked who you were, so you went home and slept so soundly that when you woke up, part of you felt like it had been carved out and lost. The point is this: Gordon is right in a way he doesn't fully understand.

Of course, you can't communicate any of this to him. You manage to say, "Not really," but how can you *not really* smoke weed? Then you just stand there literally with your dick in your hands until he whistles into the silence and leaves the bathroom without using the sink.

Gordon isn't in psychology class for the next two weeks. You start to doubt if he's real, until one day you are walking up Arkansas Avenue and see him standing alone in the yard of an ivy-covered house. He is bent over a long piece of jagged cardboard, which he has made into a sign affixed to wooden stakes. He is hammering it into the grass with rusty garden shears.

You step into the yard and read the sign, which says THE MASSES ARE THE OPIATE OF THE MASSES in permanent marker. Gordon doesn't acknowledge you. "Where have you been?" you say.

He looks up. "Who the hell are you?"

"Eli. We have psych."

He pulls his long blond hair behind his ear and searches your face. "I have a 98 percent in that class and realized I could skip the last two weeks and still get an A." He goes back to hammering the sign for a few moments, not really making any progress. Then he drops the shears. "Want to come in?"

Behind the house, it looks like someone tried to move in years ago and gave up halfway. There's a dead potted plant sitting on a card table, a dog kennel filled with paint cans, wooden dining chairs, and furniture foam everywhere, packed into corners like snow drifts.

Gordon kicks open a side door and you follow. There's a flatscreen TV, an old rifle laid across a beanbag chair, and a fainting couch made of black shag carpet. Gordon pulls a giant dictionary from a bookshelf and opens it. The inside has been carved out and now cradles a large bag of vacuum-packed, iridescent pot.

"I just got this today," he says with barely concealed excitement. "Got a connection at the law school mailroom, which bypasses commercial shipping security. You know anyone who wants to buy some?"

"No."

"Don't you have any friends?" Gordon walks into the kitchenette and opens the package with a chef's knife. "I guess I don't either. This town is full of assholes." He comes back into the living room holding a resin-stained, neon-green bong and sits next to you on the black couch. "Relax. It looks suspicious if people come inside for short periods of time, anyways."

An hour later, you're fused to the couch and Gordon has changed into a spandex biking outfit and motorcycle goggles. He looks like a vintage scuba diver as he explains how agrochemical companies want to make the next generation of men infertile.

You wish you could talk as freely as Gordon, but you haven't said much. You start to wonder if Gordon is like a bat or a dolphin—if he only knows his place in the world by how his own voice sounds when it echoes back to him.

"What's your impression of Dr. Fern?" is your best effort.

"What?"

"Like—I don't know. What's up with that little fan she takes everywhere?"

"I have one word for that," says Gordon. He gets up and takes several steps away from you, back turned. Then he turns around sharply. "Menopause!" he sings, like it's the hook in a Broadway musical, complete with jazz fingers.

You laugh, at first just because it's funny. But then you laugh for so long that you are laughing for a different reason. All the depictions of getting high you've seen are like this. Maybe you and Gordon are laughing to fit a preordained vision of what high people do. Maybe you are laughing to become who you want to be. And who is that?

You want to integrate with the world. You want to be reinvented by someone else's glow. You don't want to sit on couches and stare at potential friends like some kind of teenage Queen Victoria. But the problem is that you've learned never to trust the work that would get you there. Even if you were to able get in touch with yourself, your worry is that you don't have a self worth relating to.

Then Gordon is back on the couch. He has a brown plush blanket draped over his head, beneath which you can hear the rip of the bong. Smoke comes out of the top like a volcano. You stand up.

"Gordon, I'm going to tell you something, and I want you to promise you won't treat me differently afterward."

You pace the floor like a dog without a bed.

"I'm fucked up," you say.

The volcano starts nodding. "Yeah," it says.

"No, you don't get it. My life is shit, and I'm starting to wonder if I need to just burn it all down. Maybe then it will make some kind of sense."

Gordon does not respond. The volcano stops spewing.

"Can you see anything from under that blanket?"

"Nope."

You walk over to the beanbag chair and pick up the hunting rifle. You nestle the butt into your shoulder and point the barrel straight at Gordon's head. You open the breech. There's no round. You push the bolt forward.

"What was that sound?"

You put the gun back on the chair. "My mother died when I was twelve," you blurt out. "Some drunk bitch drove her into a semi truck."

At this point, you pause, because you know deep down that your mother's death is barely related to the inner turmoil you were trying to air. But this is the only badge of victimhood you know how to wear, so you continue. "She died, and everything that happened afterward seems like a nightmare. I don't know what's worse—living at home and being reminded of her every day, or moving to college where no one knows, then starting to doubt if it's even real. If it's just something I made up."

Gordon slips the blanket off his face, looking about as sober as someone can in a bike suit and goggles. He hunches over, starts wringing his hands. "Damn, dude."

You sit there and stare at each other for a long time, listen to half of a song from a car blaring pop radio at an intersection outside. Eventually, Gordon gets up and turns on the TV, hands you a game controller.

"What's this?"

"This is me, not treating you differently."

Soon you are a pink cartoon blob holding a samurai sword, and you are fighting a dinosaur with a laser gun. You already feel better, despite the fact that no one understands how you feel, that no one really heard you. In the end, this will be a place the newspapers

and attorneys come back to when they want to paint you as a misanthrope, to magnify your marginality. They will say that you be-
friended a drug dealer, that you were addicted to violent video games.
Of course, people will do whatever they can to believe that you were
only battling yourself, that you alone were responsible for the opposing dependencies within you that met like colliding fires.

But when I think of you sitting on Gordon's couch, you are still
just a candidate. You haven't killed anyone, and you're not even planning to. You are not yet the apoplectic shithead you will later become, who we will decide is not worth understanding. Sure, you have
made a few bad choices. You have acquired limitations. And you are
heading down a road that eventually leads to a dead end. But at this
point, there are a few arterial roads. And as far as I'm concerned, one
of those roads is Gordon.

But you didn't exactly plan out this whole "making a friend" thing.
The semester is over, and you have five days to move all your shit out
of the dorms and drive back to your father's house in Earl Heights.
You are supposed to work a summer job so you can help pay for next
year's tuition. But you haven't looked, except that one day you went
on jobhunter.com and found a posting for Larry's Hot Dog Stand,
then closed your laptop.

You don't know what to do, so you do nothing. You walk by
Gordon's house a few times but you don't see him. You sit in your
dorm and watch as the station wagons arrive. The dumpsters fill up
with cheap lamps and kitschy posters of European landmarks. You
wait until all the music stops, and when you step out into the hallway, all you can see is a whorl of light coming from the open door
of the resident assistant's room. Campus is overrun by birds and the
violent buzzing of cicadas. You watch porn and read short stories.
Eventually, the world feels so empty that the silence grows into something that has a shape, and you are the only one left who can feel it.

Then the RA knocks on your door. You don't answer, so he leaves and comes back with a master key. He steps in and regards the semi-circle of books and clothes around your bed, the plates of half-eaten cafeteria food, the sports car calendar that still sits at January.

"You were supposed to be out of here yesterday," he says. "What's your handicap?" He has a shaved head and gigantic blue eyes that make him look like a toddler.

"I decided to stay."

"Do you have somewhere to go?"

"I decided to stay."

The face he makes is one you've seen often. He looks like he just got stabbed and can't feel the knife. You stare at that face until he leaves, then you sit back down at your desk like a poor imitation of Bartleby the Scrivener.

Two hours later, your father shows up. He's wearing a pit-stained T-shirt and jeans encrusted with sawdust, so you know he came directly from work. He takes one look at your room, goes downstairs, and comes back with an armful of cardboard boxes. He starts packing. For a moment, you sit there defiantly. But then you remember you have no leverage over someone who knows all your erstwhile afflictions, who would regard your distress as something small and unspectacular.

So you pack up, follow your father's truck in your BMW beyond Ozarka and toward gently sloping plains and loblolly pine forests. You are headed to Earl Heights, a once prosperous town whose bucolic virtues have been scattered by chain stores and a uranium plant. Your father lives down in a valley tucked away from the traffic. To get there, you drive on winding roads past new subdivisions that look shadowed and evil against the cows and hayfields. Every morning, a man everyone calls "Stocky" can be seen running laps around the town, charging up hills shirtless, a huge swastika tattooed between his shoulder blades.

But before you get home, your father pulls into Elephant Ed's, the main gathering spot in town aside from Wal-Mart and the parking lot of Whirlie's auto shop. The two of you sit at the lunch counter and eat pulled pork and potato salad, staring at un-ironic cat portraits and high school memorabilia on the wall. A portrait of Ronald Reagan has a note taped to its frame: NOT FOR SALE.

"Must be hard coming back here after living in the city."

"It's not really a city."

Your father leans over the counter and gets in your face, so you are forced to make eye contact. Once you look at him, he leans back and continues to eat. "Don't take this the wrong way," he says, "but I asked around about a summer job for you. My buddy Ramon works for Butler Chicken. He's got a side job. Needs help tomorrow."

In between flipping houses, your father sometimes puts on clean work clothes and steps onto half-built tract housing and asks the construction workers if they need another hand. This, you surmise, is how he knows a guy named Ramon.

"Sounds good?"

"Sounds like a mindless summer job."

"A mindless summer job," he enunciates, "will help you see how some people have to work to survive. So when you get a career, you're able to sympathize with the continuing reality of other people's lives. So you'll regard us not with pity but with respect." Your father waves his hand around the restaurant, toward the kitchen and waitstaff, as he says this. He's talking like he has an audience, though he doesn't. "Menial labor can be edifying. College ain't gonna teach you that."

"Okay—are you done?"

"Yeah, man. I'm done."

Your father is right, of course, but the problem with getting a job now is you feel shamed into it. Even if you were to show up and work hard, it would no longer be an act of pride or diligence, but the mark of some kid who is desperate to revoke his inferior status.

You leave Elephant Ed's and drive home. When you pull up, there's a woman tanning in the brown grass. She's wearing a straw cowboy hat and a blue bikini. She waves at your father's truck like she's in a parade, but when she sees your car, she stands up, takes off her hat, and clutches it to her chest with the timidity of someone who just got out of the shower. You realize this woman is Joe. She watched you a few times when you were younger, back when your father binged on the attention of women who felt sorry for him. Everyone in town knows her as the woman who plays acoustic guitar every Sunday at the farmer's market, strumming four-chord songs so simplistic and breezy it seems like she's making them up on the spot. "Summertime is fun, let's have fun in the summertime!"

Your father gets out of his truck quickly, says a few inaudible things to her before you approach. "Eli, you remember Joe," he says.

"Look at you, the prodigal son home from college," she says, clearly misappropriating that biblical allusion. If anything, you're the other son—the one who complains about not being given a goat.

"Home," you say, "is that what we're calling this?"

"I didn't plan for the two of you to be reintroduced this way," interrupts your father.

"Anyways, I was just going to leave—" Joe begins.

"No," he says, grabbing her wrist. "You should stay."

That night, you stay in your room while Joe and your father watch a movie—some Johnny Depp blockbuster from two years ago. You lie on your bed, listening to the music and muffled dialogue until it ends. The house is silent. The sky outside blushes red before it dims. Here, on a mattress shoved into the corner of your room: this is where your childhood once barreled down Old Wire Road before shattering against a bumper. Here is where you locked yourself in the bathroom like it was a chrysalis, transforming you in isolation. Here's where you became so alone that one summer day you knocked on your own front door and pretended to be someone looking for your mom.

"Hi, I'm wondering if Mrs. Habberton might be available."

"Eli, what are you doing?"

"Who is Eli?"

Here is where your father slammed the door in your face.

In the morning, you get in your car—still packed with boxes—and drive half an hour outside of Earl Heights toward a place called Aloma. You have to drive your BMW down a long stretch of bumpy county roads, while dust and barking farm dogs gather behind you. The road twists up over sandstone bluffs and pockets of shortleaf pine. You pass a decaying school bus, several church houses in disrepair. A woman holding a scruffy dog in her arms smokes a cigarette on her porch, handless.

Eventually you drive down into flat farmland interspersed with rows of chicken houses. Ramon meets you at a gate.

"You must be Danny's boy," he says.

"Yep."

"Heard you're going to OU." He pumps his fist and says "Go Racoons," like he's encouraging a small child. Then he spits some of his chew next to your car door. It stains the dust a dark inky color.

Ramon takes you inside one of the metal chicken houses. The barn curtains are drawn so there's no natural light, just huge stage lamps beaming down like you're in a demented football arena. On one side of the room, there are thousands of yellow baby chickens separated by a small fence. The other side is empty, except for a frayed office chair and a strange metal box.

"Ever work with chickens before?" Ramon says, yelling over the cacophony of chirps.

You shrug.

"Well, these guys are a day old, which means they still need to be sexed, vaccinated, and trimmed. Your job will be trimming. It's easy—just watch."

Ramon grabs a large plastic bin and steps over the gate into the field of birds. He sets the bin down, grabs a handful of chicks, and throws them into the bin. Some make it in, some don't. Once the bin is full, he brings it back over to the fence and turns on the strange metal box. It has a small, red-hot blade that slowly moves up and down, bisecting a stationary piece of metal. Ramon grabs one chick from the bin, clutching its head in his fist, then sticks about a third of its beak on the metal until the blade comes down like a guillotine and chops it off. He does this several times, dropping each chick to the floor with the indifference of someone who has done this many times.

He looks up at you, judging your hesitation. "They're going to the layer houses," he says. "Trimming makes it so they won't peck each other to death." He gives you several more tutorials before telling you all of the birds need to be trimmed today. He hands you some wool gloves, and when he opens the door to leave, it frames the sunlight in a way that makes the open air look like another dimension.

When you step over the fence, the chicks scamper away from you quicker than you expect, so you have to shovel them rapidly into the bin. You take special care with the first one you trim. You grip her head in one hand, support her body in the other. You make sure you don't cut too deep. You set her on the sawdust floor and watch her stumble away like a wind-up toy with a melted, plastic beak.

Time passes, but it's impossible to know how much. You empty several bins and the room of chicks doesn't look any different. You didn't use the gloves, so now your wrists are covered in tiny scratches. You find ways to entertain yourself. You select one chick who gets to survive. You don't trim her beak, and when Ramon opens the door to tell you it's lunchtime, you put her in your shirt and go sit in your car with the air conditioning on. You stroke her fuzzy head while you eat.

At the end of the day, Ramon says it's okay that you didn't finish all your trimming—you can come back tomorrow. No big deal.

You say you want to do one more bin, and when he leaves you search amongst the half-beaked chicks for the one you chose. It takes you twenty minutes, but you find her.

Your excitement about leaving work quickly dissipates once you remember where you are going. You are not just afraid of your father and the new arbitrariness of your home, but also of the thoughts you might have in that house by yourself. So you take your foot off the gas. You drive so slow that you have to debate whether or not to pass the tractors driving on the shoulder.

When you get home, you go into your father's room. He's not there. You find a bunch of Joe's shoes and underwear scattered on the floor. Empty cups once filled with triple screwdrivers—your father's nightly drink—are grouped on his dresser. You rummage through drawers and find several photographs of your mother. You dig deeper and find a vintage electric "back massager" and a pink ball gag. You tear through the whole house looking for something that matters, something to distract you from the summer spreading before you like an endless yellow field. Eventually, you are standing at the threshold of the bathroom. You stare at the blurry daylight spotlighting a square on the tile. You are about to get inside and never come out, but ultimately decide it is a leftover impulse from childhood. Instead, you should go out and make the world bend to your will, spare yourself from the fate of being unheard and defeated.

So this is what you do. You go back into your father's room, grab Joe's guitar by the neck, and take a swing against his bookshelf. Then you take one against his desk, his wall, his mirror, until you are out of breath and the body has detached from the strings. You put the guitar down, then get into your car and drive on the dirt road that leads away from your father's house. Then, as if realizing this moment should feel more dramatic, you drive faster, kicking up a trail of dust behind you, crashing into large divots and spraying rocks everywhere. At one point you hit a pothole so large that your bumper crunches, starts dragging on the ground until you hit another bump and there it goes, flung to the side as you fishtail around a bend. You are driving to Ozarka, and you are never coming back.

You go straight to Gordon's house. He answers the door bare-chested in a silk kimono, gripping his rifle indolently in one hand, the same way someone might hold a television remote. And when he looks over your shoulder at your bumperless car filled with junk, you realize you probably smell like sweat and chicken shit. You consider the idea that he might have seen you lurking around his house, trying to decipher light and shadows from beneath the mismatched blankets he uses for curtains.

But the thing is—you're desperate. You're like someone in debt who starts buying lottery tickets instead of declaring bankruptcy. So you invite yourself in and tell Gordon everything. Your father turned into a martinet. He replaced your dead mother with a moronic slut. He realized you are smarter than him, so he dragged you back to a one-horse town and found you the most undignified job he could. You're almost done with your rant but you stop because Gordon is still standing at the edge of the room, like you are a flare and he is trying to stay just beyond the reach of light. You look for signs of combativeness in his face, and that's when he sprays spit into the air, doubles over, and starts laughing.

"I'm sorry," he says, kneeling down to place his forehead on the edge of the couch. "I know you're going through some shit, but I'm seriously fucked up right now."

You get up and grab the bong from the kitchen counter, then open the dictionary and start loading a bowl.

"Hey," says Gordon.

You take a hit from the bong without acknowledging him, blow the smoke up toward the ceiling. "How much of this have you sold?"

"Meh."

"You should sell some before we smoke it all." You take another hit, and when you inhale the smoke you think of that first night in this apartment when you discovered that opening up to someone didn't hurt so bad, but in fact put you on the map, turned you back into a human from a shadow.

It's at this point you remember the baby chick is still in your car. You go outside, open your car door, and are greeted by a wave of heat. You dig around until you find her under the passenger seat, still alive. When you come back, you set her on Gordon's coffee table with a flourish, like you just performed a magic trick.

So you get high together, again, and it's not long before Gordon rants about how Egyptian hieroglyphs depicted modern aircraft, like helicopters and the Hubble telescope. These drawings are evidence, apparently, of how aliens built the pyramids before human civilization existed. He explains all this while clutching the baby bird to his chest like she's a tiny cat. He says you should name her Girlfriend.

At this moment, Gordon looks at you and notices you are actually smiling. It's a smile that appears to unsheathe everything about you. It makes you look like some kid in his father's work clothes who wants approval, some kid who needs a place to stay, who doesn't know where he is going, but who is willing to take everyone—including the people he loves—along with him. It is why Gordon takes a blanket from the window and tells you to go to sleep, that you can stay for as long as you need.

This is how you and Gordon end up living together. He gets a job washing dishes at the gourmet grilled cheese restaurant on the Ave, and you encourage him to sell weed to his coworkers. The two of you talk about profit margins and fronts, about scraping up enough money to buy a pound. You don't unpack your things, not even your clothes. You wear your work boots and your father's old jeans, then you go down to the thrift store and buy an army jacket. You rip all the Grateful Dead and peace sign patches from the fabric and start wearing it everywhere, defiantly sweating through it in the summer heat. You stop gelling your hair, let it grease over and hang down near your eyes like an apathetic English sheepdog. You sit at the bar waiting for Gordon's shift to end, and his coworkers serve you beer without asking for ID. The two of you sneak around town at night. You heave a sectional couch off a bridge and into a creek. You walk up to the front doors of Sigma Chi and spray paint DICK PALACE on the colonial façade.

But your father doesn't call, doesn't pay your cell phone bill. You thought your outburst was extreme enough to garner attention, but instead it hangs in the air like a picture made of smoke. You don't know how you'll pay for tuition, but you enroll for fall semester anyways. Girlfriend's feathers pale, and she grows out of her cute phase and into a dinosaur-like bird that shits every thirty minutes. Gordon locks her in the bathroom, which ruins the one place you like to hide, but you're not that person anymore. You're now living in the after-image of yourself, pushing your life forward into the future, where you're not sure it belongs.

One night, Gordon smokes too much and passes out watching "UFO Secrets of the Third Reich" on his laptop. Then the power goes out. This is a problem because you're like a shark—stop, and you suffocate. The room dislocates itself. The carpet looks like your mother's casket fabric. Memories explode like a flock of birds from a tree. So you step outside. A warm and directionless wind surges around you. Then your phone rings, and you think it might be your father, but when you answer it's a robotic voice telling you to seek shelter, because a tornado warning is in effect. Though it's the end of tornado season, the campus alert system—named, of all things, "OzAlert"—hasn't called you once. You realize this is exciting. You want to stand alone in the path of something furious.

So you find an old chair, then place it on top of a card table and climb onto Gordon's roof. Up there, you watch the shifting clouds, the black sky veined with faraway lightning, and the headlights on the freeway breaking the darkness in half. As you wait for the storm to arrive, you imagine how the clouds will gather. You see the funnel descend. Everyone runs, crawls under their houses, while barns are ripped apart and splinters of wood stab knifelike into soil. Herds of cattle leave their broken fences behind. Churches spin on their foundations. Giant bugs smash into walls like the whole town is racing down the freeway. But you are not running or hiding. You are presiding over it. You realize you want for everyone together to be torn apart, for their voices to sing and the wind to blow away your life like the extravagant sand castle that it is.

But the storm doesn't come. The power comes back on, and the lights from houses and the Super Wal-Mart float companionless in the dark. Soon the sky turns pearly with daylight, and all the green trees and dun-colored apartment complexes stretch into the hills. That's when it feels like something out there has shifted. The storm you imagined is real, even if it's only coming from within.

DECOMPOSER

ROSE

WHEN YOU RETURN TO CAMPUS after the shooting, it reminds you of Alla Vista after the tornado hit, minus the FEMA trailers and hills of splintered wood. At first, there are tiny white crosses in the grass, leaves murmuring through moments of silence, gangs of service dogs, free nutritional bars and bottled water. T-shirts and roadside cardboard say WE STAND WITH YOU or RACCOON PRIDE WILL PREVAIL, like the whole town is preparing to lose an important football game. American flags hang from fire truck ladders. Missionaries chase you down the street to hand you brochures, one of which is just a collage depicting winged lions, the president, and the devil bursting from a vortex of fire. PREPARE FOR JUDGMENT DAY, it says.

When classes begin, the language of loss is everywhere. Volunteer clinicians take the lectern, talk about transient stress reactions, survivor's guilt, recovering in the glare of the national spotlight. One of them, trying hard to talk poetically about the healing process, says that a tree takes the same amount of time to decompose as it does to grow. This notion unsettles you, because you were never taught that losses decompose—they've always hardened into something permanent. You find yourself envying the secondary victims of the shooting. After all, they are enduring tragedy together, writing poems about fugue states, visiting counselors in hotel rooms. They are not indigent survivors in a town that can barely stitch a gash on a young girl's forehead.

It's February, and winter still has you by the throat. Colors of the sky smolder against spindly trees and stone buildings. You wake up in your clothes, lines on your skin from unintended sleep. You walk by the library and regard the letters, candles, and makeshift cenotaphs like something is missing. A balloon pops in the BOK foyer, and everyone drops to the ground and covers their head except you. Eventually, some of your sisters notice your withdrawn countenance, and they ask if you know anyone who died. You tell them the wife of your English professor was killed, but that's it. You realize you are not a victim, but beyond that you just don't know anymore.

Then on the Saturday before Valentine's Day, Delta Nu decides to throw the first party since the shooting. This party is important because one of the brothers has been courting you since the school year began. His name is Brooks Fowler. He's a senior who rides around town on a scooter with studded tires and a Jesus fish mounted beneath the headlight. Despite being single, he's a Christian marriage counselor, which means he meets with other frat boys in the campus Starbucks and says "Christ chose you for one another" whenever they express doubts about their fiancés. Brooks is not exactly your type— in fact, you'll later realize he's the complete opposite of your type— but that's not the point. The point, you think, as you talk yourself into going, is that you should be grateful for the attention. You tell yourself to remember where you came from, that you graduated from a high school whose valedictorian flunked sophomore year, then you became the only pledge without legacy to be accepted by BOK. You try to remember how this is supposed to be your new family.

So you get ready for the party, using the eyeliner Drew Barrymore gave everyone the previous weekend when she visited to promote her new optical line. You adhere teeth whitening strips, comb your hair against the grain until it has so much volume it dwarfs the size of your face. Then you step out onto the street, where dried-up leaves skitter across the cement with a sound like rain. You walk down to the edge of Greek Row toward Delta Nu, a ten-thousand-square foot Civil War–era house with stone turrets, the same house that hosts Miss Arkansas contestants in the summer. When you get inside, the beer is still cold and foamless. There's no dance music stealing conversation, just some girl who keeps sneaking up to the iPod and playing Brad Paisley's "American Saturday Night." There are no strobe lights or bubble machines, no one getting dared to swallow goldfish, offering you drinks from a suspicious gas station slushy machine, pointing to your torso and saying, "How can you have body image issues with a body like that?" It's just you in the parlor, talking to Ashley beneath a composite photo of alumni.

Ashley is telling you about what happened last week, how someone climbed to the top of the library and hung a large banner from the side that said WE FORGIVE YOU, ELI. How the mother of one of the victims, upset by this knee-jerk Christian reaction, went to go take it down but fell off the ladder and broke her ankle. How a local pastor took to his pulpit, told everyone to focus on his or her own sins to shed corrosive anger, then went home and drank a cup of bleach to cleanse himself and slipped into a coma. You already know all this happened, but you let Ashley tell you anyway.

Then a guy named Johnny comes down the stairs. He's wearing a paisley shirt and a captain's hat, carries a ukulele in one hand. "Hold on," he says, stepping between you and Ashley. "You guys can't be talking about this stuff here. It's a party—we're supposed to be having fun." He lifts the ukulele up and uses it as a back scratcher.

You consider changing the subject, but you're tired of guys trying to impress you by telling you to shut up.

"I don't know," you continue. "I keep thinking it's absurd to argue about what the shooting means, because maybe there is no meaning. Telling Eli we forgive him? That's like pardoning a storm."

No one responds. Ashley swirls her near-empty cup. This is a red light/green light party, meaning you wear green if you're single and red if you're taken. You are wearing a black low-cut blouse tucked into a green body-con skirt. Johnny's shirt is yellow.

"Very clever," you say, pointing to his shirt. You figure he's wearing it for some snarky-ass reason, and you don't want to give him the satisfaction of telling you.

"Can you play a song on that thing?" says Ashley.

Johnny positions the ukulele at his chest and strums a bright, islandy chord. "Come outside with me," he says, but he's only looking at you. He grabs your hand and leads you outside. You look back over your shoulder and watch Ashley disappear.

You go out to a balcony that overlooks a volleyball court and Delta Nu's private parking lot full of trucks and midsize SUVs.

"I totally agree with you—by the way," says Johnny. "My father used to say that people embrace forgiveness so they can pretend the world is more just than it actually is."

You like that idea, but you also know that the best way to talk to a pushy guy like this is to neither affirm nor deny that moral facts exist. "Yeah," you say, "but sometimes I worry that if life has no value, all is just."

"Just what?"

You pat Johnny on the head like he's a sweet dog. "Never mind," you say. He ignores your touch and starts playing his ukulele.

"Look at the stars," he sings, "look how they shine for you. They were all yellow." It's a song everyone is tired of, but he croons it slow like Roy Orbison, and you figure it relates to his shirt, but you're not sure in what way. As he sings, you wait for an irony that never quite appears.

"Shut up, faggot!" screams someone from down in the parking lot. Johnny does not yell back or throw anything. He just shakes his head in disappointment. This, you think, is a sign that he is a good person.

You go back inside, play drinking games on the dirty floor. You talk to Johnny about religion, tell him about the pastor's son who took you into a back room when you were eleven and told you to stop being a glutton and a temptress, who later rode his dirt bike to your house and wouldn't stop grabbing your hair. You show him a picture on your phone of a woman in Wal-Mart wearing a shirt that says LIFE IS BETTER WITH JESUS AND SANDALS. Johnny sets down his ukulele. He listens, and it's nice because it has been a long time since you could talk honestly without fearing social retribution.

Eventually, all the beer is gone, and the party has moved into the basement where it's dark enough to dance. But you're still upstairs. You've been worried all night that Brooks will show up, that he'll see you with Johnny and call you a tease or a stuck-up bitch. You are standing in the potent kitchen lights, thinking the party has no more lastingness, when Johnny grabs you by the arm.

"I have more beer downstairs," he says.

"I don't need anymore," you say, but he's already pulling you across the foyer and opening a door. You are stomping down steep wooden stairs in your wedge heels, realizing this is not the dance party. You're pulled past small, blacked-out windows, laundry machines, and old mops in five-gallon buckets. Then through a hallway of curtains, behind which is a small room filled with lofted beds, a fridge, and an entertainment center. You are sitting on one of the beds, holding another beer but not drinking it, watching the latter half of an Andy Kaufman movie. Dance music still pulverizes the walls, but trying to find out where it's coming from would be like looking for a jet based on the thrum of the engine cutting through the sky.

Johnny takes out his phone and points it at you. You're able to put your hand over your face before the camera's flash fills the room.

"Don't," you say.

Johnny laughs. "Check it out," he says, leaning over to show you the picture. Your green skirt does look strangely vibrant against his black comforter, but he has already put a filter over it, saturating all the colors.

"I don't like when a photo is so obviously edited," you say. "It looks so contrived."

From here, you and Johnny debate photography. "Since everything is digital, there's no purity left," he says. "Filters are just the way things look now."

You try to stay attentive, but the argument goes on much longer than you want, and you sink farther into the bed, feeling the cool and deep and vibrating house surround you.

When you open your eyes, Johnny is above you, hands on your shoulders. You look into his face, but it's half wiped out by darkness, a new distance in his eyes. He pushes you down into the bed until it feels like you're going to be spit out on the other side. Only one of your shoes is on. He kisses you with an open mouth, brackish with spit and alcohol. "I want to fuck you," he says.

You do not pull away or say anything, because you sense that what he said is not a request, that it's his way of telling you what is about to happen. Somewhere along the way, an agreement was made that you were not a part of. And you figure resisting leads to the same outcome, since you're dealing with someone who is locked so completely within the oblivion of his own pride and comfort that he has already glossed over your fear as if it were coquettishness. "Why you squirming like a scalded dog?" This is why you decide the only way out is through, that surrendering is the only way to exercise what little choice you have been given. So that's what you do.

After pretending to sleep for a few hours, you leave and walk back to your dorm room alone. For some reason, it doesn't seem like anything terrible has happened, even though everything is wrong. Any words or explanations you use, attempting to frame the situation, immediately distance you from the experience as it has been lived. It's almost as if the longer you keep it lodged in that sub rosa part of your mind, the less likely it will be to enter the realm of meaning. So you get into your car. You drive west on the homogenous freeway all night, stop at a gas station in north Texas when the sky begins bursting with light, where all you can see for miles is grass and a crooked water tower. Out here, the land is so flat that you could watch someone run away for several days. Then you drive back to Ozarka, sleep through the afternoon, then wake up and drive east, through corridors of trees and stars gleaming with particularity, and in the morning you're in a town with no radio stations or grocery stores, just churches that look like old barns and a billboard that says DIVERSITY IS A CODE WORD FOR WHITE GENOCIDE. You wanted to get so lost that you could return to your original self, but it doesn't work that way. When you turn around, nothing is behind you.

The next day, you borrow your roommate's bicycle, ride north on the bike trail past schoolyards, scampering rabbits, over bridges that ice in the night. The trail ends and you pedal farther, past the gravel pits and bodegas of Hilldale, end up on the backside of the Super Wal-Mart. It's three thirty in the morning. You step inside, wander isles of Ozarka Raccoon beer koozies and stuffed animals, glass cases of ammunition, pyramids of flawless vegetables. Then you are in the freezer section, staring at a wall of packaged corn dogs, feeling the machines hum in your chest. You look into the glass and find a clear reflection of a girl wearing no makeup, hair flattened from her helmet, floating on the white tile like she's entering another dimension. You do this for a long time, and when you leave without buying anything, and the sun has come up, and your phone is dead and you barely know how to get home, you realize you found a place that matches the dislocation you feel inside.

You do this for three nights in a row, skipping all your classes. You don't go to the cafeteria, subsist on the box of stale nut bars and instant coffee that your foster mother gave you back in August. Then one night, you're riding through a stretch of forest between unkempt townhouses when you see a kitten skulking in the frozen bramble. It exerts a long, pitiable meow. You don't stop. Instead, you continue on your way to Wal-Mart and buy red nail polish that you will never use because you associate it with this time in your life. On your ride back you see the kitten again. It looks straight at you and meows, eyes dime-like in the dark. Again, you do nothing. You keep riding home. And when you get there, you cry. You wonder why you are a terrible person, why you're giving up your ability to be normal, moving into an abyss of anger and fear that could be avoided, if you just knew how to move on.

Thunderclouds fill the sky. Streets turn into rivers of rushing water and trash. Umbrellas are useless. Classes canceled. It rains so hard that a quarter mile of the bike trail falls down an embankment. Tree branches cough up onto front lawns like driftwood. So you're forced to stay inside. You read clickbait articles, watch videos on dopecatgallery.com, sign a petition to shut down SeaWorld. Then you start looking at personal ads. You read through all the desperate paragraphs. The people who ask outright to be saved from their loneliness, who want Asian girlfriends, mature men with big wangs, who aren't afraid to tell the world I LIKE NURSING ON A TITS. They ask, is there life after love? Where have all the cowboys gone? You used to do this for a laugh, but now you see a blazing humanness in their dejection. You want to call these people and give them whatever they want, turn your sadness into a superpower. At one point, you almost contact a man who is looking for a young girl with cute feet, but you come to your senses. So you keep scrolling, looking for something—you're not sure what.

This is how you meet Ellen. She posts in the W4W section, saying she's a volunteer photographer for families with terminally ill babies, needs an assistant to come with her to the hospital, hold light boxes and reflectors. She says she needs someone who is calm, who can keep her company on the drive home. "You have to understand," she writes, "that there is no tomorrow for these families."

So you contact her, exchange emails. She tells you about anencephaly, tubal litigations, myopathy. Says she was adopted from the Dominican Republic by Christian missionaries, homeschooled all her life, and never went to college. You tell her about sorority life, classes, how lately you've been spending your days with headphones in, lying in tanning beds and waiting for the blue light to annihilate your afternoon. You start to believe you've found a companion, have fantasies about riding off toward the grey skies together. You put on regular clothes and go to class. You buy a sandwich and eat it outside.

Eventually, Ellen starts getting hospital referrals, so you leave campus and don't tell anyone where you're going. You drive to her apartment, on the backside of a faded beige complex where the sidewalks are strewn with cheap barbecues and plastic children's toys. She doesn't invite you in, just unlatches the array of deadbolts from inside and squeezes out onto the concrete like there's some giant monster she's leaving behind. The first time you show up, she's wearing a black trench coat and stark white sneakers. Horn-rimmed glasses adorn her small-featured face.

"Suddenly, I feel like I'm taking you out on the most depressing date ever," she says.

"But you look so nice."

She gives you a disapproving scowl. "Thanks."

So you drive to Mercy, Levi County, Baptist Memorial. You roll the windows down, watch the roadside grass sway in the shifting winds, let the noise of the freeway block out the talk radio, which is once again saying "The Ozarka shooting was the second most deadly in state history," like it's a goddamn record to be broken. On the way, Ellen teaches you about apertures, shutter speeds, flash triggers, lenses. She asks about the scar on your head and you don't lie. You don't say "bike accident" or "Marry Poppins imitation." You tell her what a mattress looks like when it goes cartwheeling into a roofless sky.

"I'm here anytime you want to talk about it," she says. It is a comment you find remarkable for how affirming it is, in all its simplicity.

The hospitals spread across farmland like misplaced airports, clean windows reflecting the cheery blue sky. They look like megachurches with big crosses and Jesus statues big as dinosaurs. When you step inside, nurses brief you on the condition of each baby. They have been alive six days. They can't breathe or swallow on their own. They have heart defects, spent months with umbilical cords wrapped around their necks. They have underdeveloped cerebellums. They are about to be given medication so they feel no pain when unhooked from their machines.

The first family you work with shows a certain joy in the ceremony, seems prepared to cross the channel that will redefine their pain. They wear church clothes. When they unhook their baby from the machine, it doesn't feel like someone just died in the room, and they don't seem plagued by this ambiguity. They hold him like he is still alive. The mother takes off her shirt and touches skin to skin, poses for Ellen like a Madonna with ribbons of light and riots of flowers behind her. After this, they invite their entire family in the room, teenagers and grandparents and everyone, chins pointed down at the baby being held like a book everyone is trying to read at the same time.

The second family greets you hunched in the corner, wearing pit-stained T-shirts and hospital gowns. They hold the baby like it's a fragile carving, and it's so quiet you can hear its mechanized breathing. They stare straight at the camera, shadows stabbing onto the walls behind them. And when you move toward them with reflectors, something strange in the room seems to be absorbing all the light. Ellen doesn't take as many pictures, packs up her camera bag. "I'm sorry this happened to you," she says, then makes arrangements to send the prints. While you wait for the elevator, you see the nurse carry the body back to the neonatal intensive care unit.

"This is hard," you say. "You can't really take these moments back."

"That's pretty much all of photography," says Ellen, though she has to know you weren't just talking about pictures.

One day, you are driving back from a hospital when Ellen takes her eyes off the road and looks straight at you. She asks if you want to come home and stay the night with her. She broke up with her boyfriend, who moved out a month ago, but he's still "at large"—whatever that means. "I can't sleep," she says. "I just lie awake, waiting for a knock at my door."

"Of course," you say. "No problem." You say this not only because you want to help, but because for the past month, you've only been able to sleep in the afternoon, when your roommate is in class and sunlight seeps through the mini-blinds and turns the whole room bright gray. Otherwise, you fall asleep and wake up in an impersonal basement, no air or sound until you see Johnny's face and the scene boils over in your mind. Or you lie awake thinking about the kitten on the bike trail. You still feel like it is out there, waiting for you.

There is no furniture in Ellen's apartment, just a mattress on the floor, a few boxes of clothing, and a television hooked up to a Nintendo. The sink is filled with dirty dishes and the carpet is matted with animal hair, despite no animals being around. You follow Ellen into the kitchen and she opens a beer for you without asking. She goes into her room and comes back having changed into exercise shorts and a black T-shirt that says FEAR NO MAN. She gives you pajama pants and a shirt with a giant wolf head on the front, surrounded by thunderbolts.

The two of you sit together on the floor in the living room and flip through nature documentaries, BBC adaptations of novels you've never read, Korean game shows. You finish a six-pack, then break into Ellen's random assortment of hard liquor. Eventually, she turns on the Nintendo and you take turns playing a strange Japanese adventure game. You're a mouse, and your goal is to roll everything up into a ball. You start out rolling crumbs, trash, and household items. When the ball gains mass and momentum, you start to gather cars, people, and small trees.

At one point during Ellen's turn, you go into the kitchen for another drink and find one of her photography portfolios on the counter behind an old toaster. The first picture you flip to is a close-up of a baby's foot, cupped by two separate hands, wedding rings dulled by the sepia tones you've heard families ask for, hoping for that heirloom quality.

You walk back into the living room. "What got you into hospital photography?"

"I guess it's a great thing to do for people," Ellen says, still mashing buttons on the controller. "But honestly I'm trying to get experience so I can make money doing wedding photography. A dramatic transition, but death is the mother of beauty."

This last statement sounds like something Eddie would have said in English class. "I like the way that sounds," you say, then you repeat it. "Death is the mother of beauty."

Ellen laughs. "It's from a poem," she says. "And whatever you do, don't say that at the hospital."

"Why not?"

"Because people don't want their pain to be explained away like that. They want to embrace it." Ellen starts picking up large buildings with the ball, but accidentally rolls it into a canyon. "Damn it," she says as the screen flashes GAME OVER and the mouse hangs its head in disappointment.

You think of what the clinician said, how recovery is waiting for something within you to decompose, and you think that Ellen is right. What kind of person is going to be reassured by a slogan?

You think about this until you go to bed and Ellen puts her arms around you and rests her head on your shoulder, and together you both wait for a knock that never comes, and when you fall asleep, you dream for the first time in months. You dream you are a mouse rolling houses and landmarks up into a ball, and you get so much momentum that you roll over states and continents. You're in outer space collecting planets, the blinding light of celestial bodies.

It's not long before you're spending most nights at Ellen's, borrowing her clothes and buying furniture for her apartment together, sneaking into the back doors of dive bars, coming back smelling like cigarettes and stale beer and feeling the warmth of each other's bodies. You keep going to class but you don't talk to anyone. You avoid every party bus and BOK social. You don't go to the Chamelionare concert. You don't dress up for bowling night and pile into the back of a pickup, surrounded by platinum hair flapping in the wind. You don't show up for the BOK recruitment video, gather beneath a rented drone, laugh in a white dress, and blow glitter in your sisters' faces. You don't dance with Ricky Raccoon at midfield in Butler Chicken Stadium.

Inevitably, you get kicked out, and on the day your big sister contacts you to let you know that "It's just not working out," you call Ellen. The two of you ride your bikes down into a valley on the south side of town with a bottle of wine. You pass nondescript warehouses, giant horses leaning over tiny fences, you keep your lips tight so bugs just smash against your cheeks and forehead. It's springtime now, and the hills stab into the blue sky with their total greenness. Eventually, you park your bikes at a defunct water reservoir. It's hot for this time of year, and two young boys sit in a tree above the water. One of them takes a bottle of orange soda from his bag and pours it on his head. A television sits on river rocks at the base of the dam, its screen impaled by a giant tree branch.

Ellen turns away from the water, points her camera at the rolling hills, and snaps a picture. "Did you know these are some of the oldest mountains in the country?" she says. "The reason they are so small is that they've been worn down by time."

You decide they're beautiful, and it's nice to have such a simple, unadulterated thought.

The two of you will spend the rest of the afternoon drinking wine on the top of the fragmented dam. And before you leave, Ellen will take a picture of you standing there, walls of shale and thick wilderness behind you, water cascading over your bare feet and into the obfuscated air. Your arms will be crossed over your borrowed T-shirt, some death metal band surrounded by ravens. And when Ellen develops the photo, she will retouch it using the same process she uses for remembrance photography. She will frame it and hang it on the wall in her living room. You will be drawn toward it every time you visit. The bandana tied around your greasy hair, the satisfied look on your face, your borrowed and ill-fitting clothing. The first time you see it, you will look past your perfunctory smile and find something familiar there, moving just beyond your eyes—something you have not seen in quite some time.

HOW TO FALL IN LOVE

EDDIE

CASEY IS EIGHT DAYS LATE, and the two of you are driving past the edge of Ozarka, where the frenzied scramble of housing developments flatten into monoculture, windmill farms, and broken-down trucks bulging with weeds. A mass of poetry books has accumulated on your feet, their pages folded by your shuffling legs. Soon you will be driving past Damascus, a town that was leveled by a tornado two days ago. You are looking at pictures of the storm on your phone. Dark horizon of bare trees. Crumbled subdivisions dotted with blue tarps. There's a video of the tornado positioned over the town like a column, until it shrinks and spins faster, like an ice skater pulling in her arms at the end of a twirl.

But the sky is clearing up. Two sheets of clouds pull away from the sun like parting curtains. Casey tells you that tornadoes never hit the same place twice, that they are actually pretty amazing. We would love them if they were just someplace else, she says.

You want to say that tornadoes are indifferent to what suffers. For example, a motorbike smashing through some lady's storm shelter door, winds ripping her up into the sky. That's not beauty. That's mindless malignancy. But you don't say this, because that's how so many of your pointless arguments begin, when you invent a fork in the road just because you're afraid of one appearing.

When the two of you actually drive past Damascus, there's just a bunch of negligible debris on the side of the road. A sign for Maca-doodles Liquor hangs askew. Houses are missing roof shingles. You are not stuck in traffic because the asphalt has been ripped from the ground. Soon the town is just a sign in your rearview mirror. You're heading east on I-40, past tiny rivers and auto auctions. A billboard brags BUY A DIAMOND, GET A FREE SHOTGUN!

Just after the sun goes down, you park outside The Chalet Inn on the outskirts of West Memphis. It's a one-story motel surrounded by muddy trucks. Several men loiter outside, drinking beer under floodlights that carve hard shadows onto their faces. You can tell by looking at the place that even the non-smoking rooms will have yellow ceilings.

"Only one left has two twin beds," says the man at the front desk. He is speaking from behind a scratched-up glass partition. "All these guys working on the windmill farm up north. Been here two weeks."

"Are the beds coin-operated?" says Casey.

He doesn't answer, just chews his gum at her.

"Like, when you put quarters in the beds and they rumble around?"

"No."

"We'll take it." Casey slams down her credit card on the counter like she's just struck a deal.

Once inside, Casey drops her bag and jumps onto one of the beds, smiling. A mirror that spans the entire wall makes it seem like there is another room beyond this one. On the other wall hang two pastel blobs that barely resemble sailboats.

"Isn't this exciting?" she says.

"I guess."

She untucks the floral comforter and tosses it into the air. "Think about it," she says. "This is how married couples used to sleep a long time ago. If you were going to have sex, one of you had to get up and sneak into the other's bed. Think about the anticipation."

"I see what you mean."

Already, you can tell how lucky you are to be far from home, where familiarity grinds away at your marriage until there's no truth left in it. Just two weeks ago, you left after an argument and rolled your car on a hairpin turn in the national forest, trying to prove that you were angry, or you were sorry—you're still not sure. But now, Casey is looking at you from atop this bed. The fluorescent light reveals freckles beneath her eyes and on her shoulders, left over from summer. You let go of your worries. After all, you're the type of person who gets an odd feeling in his chest and immediately thinks of heart failure, never just acid reflux or seasonal allergies. You always blow things out of proportion.

So this is what you do. You take the tortillas, beans, and salsa from the car and make burritos in the tiny microwave. You watch television and eat. There's a recurring commercial advertising a summer country music festival, where bands play on a stage before the Mississippi River, sunburned fans cheering from their floatation devices. The color on the TV is distorted, a moderate shade of purple washing over you. Then you read poetry on the floor in this uneven light, already believing this trip will be something the two of you will enjoy retelling to each other, some years into the future.

When you go to bed, you wait for as long as you can. Outside, truck doors slam, laborers snicker into the night. The bruised moon comes in through the cheap curtains, spattering light into the room that reflects in the mirror. You keep looking at yourself, pretending your life has transferred to another dimension. You watch that other Eddie shuffle across the thin carpet and press into Casey, burying his face in her neck.

The rest passes through you like a dream. There is no room to change positions, no light for looking around. And when you finish, you do not think of its implications because you already convinced yourself Casey is pregnant and—for the moment—you want to prove you're not scared. You don't sleep much because you stay with her in the small bed, your head on her shoulder/armpit. You are awake, thinking of a tornado that doesn't destroy a thing.

The reason you're here is because you volunteered to teach poetry to fifth-graders at West Memphis Elementary. The program, which is funded by Ozarka University, pays you five hundred dollars plus travel expenses, which is more than half of your monthly paycheck. It was founded in the seventies, shortly before all the white people un-enrolled their kids from public schools, then put them in private Christian ones so they could disdain science and teach revisionist Southern history in peace.

In any case, elementary kids act the same everywhere. Their interests align with their parents'. They write poems about dead cousins. They sneak toilet humor into odd corners of their stories. They all put their mouths entirely around the water fountain spigot. The difference is their surroundings. Either they have up-to-date technology, teachers who spent time in the Peace Corps, and after-school programs, or they have animals living in their walls, fields of mud for playgrounds, laminated posters of Abe Lincoln yellowed and curling at the edges. West Memphis Elementary is the latter.

Somehow, you sleep through your alarm, and all the trucks rumble out of the parking lot without a sound. You wake up late. While Casey is in the shower, you scope out the continental breakfast, but when you get to the lobby, all you see is a giant jar of Froot Loops and pot of stagnant coffee that smells like burnt vinegar. A man with a shaved head and partially unbuttoned overalls shovels some cereal into a plastic tub, which he has brought just for the occasion.

When you leave The Chalet Inn, Casey stops at Burger King on the way into town, and you buy some kind of extreme egg sandwich.

Halfway through your meal, a semitrailer load of chickens on its way to the food processing plant pulls in front of you. Feathers bulge from the wire cages stacked on top of each other like bricks, making you wish you'd just eaten the Froot Loops. Already, you are afraid that what you felt last night was temporary. You fear that your surety will slip away if you don't keep replaying that moment in your head. You know you can't return to a feeling, but you can return to the thing that made you feel it.

The parking lot of the school is strewn with fallen trees leftover from the storm, and there's a pond-sized puddle blocking the entrance. Inside, all the kids' shoes squeak on the tiles. You and Casey stick nametags to your chests in the front office before following your guide to the classroom, where kids are lining up at the pencil sharpener. A reproachful woman makes announcements over the intercom. Thirty tiny voices shout the Pledge of Allegiance.

The teacher who invited you here is Ms. Emily Cole, a white girl in her twenties with gigantic boobs and a nose ring. On her desk, she has a framed photograph of her pet Corgi sleeping on a yellow velvet couch. The bell rings and you begin your routine. "What can a poem be about?" Thankfully, Emily doesn't zone out or use this time to grade papers, because there's one kid who keeps interjecting, "You know what?" Your first instinct is to think it's cute, and to be glad there's a student so eager. But all the children ignore his irrelevant stories. He's not even a dunce—he's a pariah. He only shuts up when Emily kneels before him and speaks to him in whispers that no one else can hear. The kid's name is Benny.

You teach three different classrooms of fifth-graders before lunch. Casey has them write about the color gold and family members. You ask them to pretend they are thirty years old. "I'm so old now," a kid laments, "I need a cane." At lunch, you and Casey sit on a rotten picnic table that overlooks the playfield, which is surrounded by a chain-link fence tall enough for a prison. Most of the kids are just screaming, though a few are running around the perimeter of the field like they're in a track meet.

"Did poets ever come to your school?" you ask.

Casey looks up into the sky for a long time, takes a bite of her gas station sandwich. "I can't remember."

"I can't either."

"What I can remember," she says, "is this one guest speaker. We were told she was an activist, but she looked like someone's mom—blond hair like a church bell, those exercise pants. Anyways, I don't remember what she said, but she gave out plastic baby figurines. Supposed to be twelve-week gestational fetuses. But they were just shrunken humans. They had eyebrows, and they were furrowing them. And I'm not sure if this is true, but I remember every kid was given a fetus, and that they had holes in their butts. I have this image of the entire class taking notes with anti-abortion pencil erasers."

Casey says all of this like it has no relation to what might be going on inside of her. She does not search your face for a reaction. She is always demonstrating how calmness begets power.

When you turn to her, the wind blows hair across her face, but behind it you know she is smiling. There are no clouds, and the sky is blue and capacious. On the field, a football game has emerged, which is basically one boy holding the ball while others surround him and shout "Throw it!" or "Get him!"

It is this moment, years later, you will come back to when you explain to me that you started seeing advance warnings of Casey's death. Underlying certain moments in the last week of her life, you experienced a happiness so strong you knew it was terminal, like when something burns so bright that you're waiting for it to explode. You will tell me this feeling was so convincing that when the bell rang and all the kids ran back into the building, you tried to stay there on the planks of the picnic table, watching as Casey packed up all the lunch garbage, then pulled you away.

When the school day ends, both of you are exhausted, but the sun is still shining, so you drive across the Mississippi River to downtown Memphis. You walk around Beale Street, eat barbeque burgers and potato salad in a dark restaurant with photographs of Elvis covering the walls. You want to have a drink outside, so you go to a patio bar called Sniffy's, which claims to be WHERE EVERY DAY IS ST. PATRICK'S DAY. You order two house specialties, which is just beer with a shot of grenadine. You drink them in wrought-iron chairs that straddle the last strip of evening sun.

Casey has been quiet since leaving the school, and she's had trouble making the simplest decisions, like what side of the table to sit on. "What are we going to do?" she says.

"I thought you didn't want to talk about it."

"Yeah, but I feel like we have been talking about it. Even though we haven't said anything."

You've been married four years now, and what you've learned is that, when the two of you have to choose between two equally difficult paths, pushing strongly for one will make you responsible for the future. You know that a certain grateful indifference is necessary for two people to feel like they've made a decision together. You can't swim out of the riptide by yourself.

"Here's what I think," you say. "I think I'll always be imagining a second life alongside my own, no matter what we do. The kid will be there, even if it isn't. And so will the absence of the kid. That will be there, too." You've finished your drink by now, but you're still putting the empty cup to your mouth.

"In either of these possible futures, can you picture yourself happy?"

"In both."

On a stage in the corner, a band starts playing an Otis Redding song, and the singer nails it with his Sunday choir-honed chops. His throaty wail isolates itself against the minor 9 keyboards and a cross stick drumbeat. You listen for a few more songs until realizing the bar is crowded. You can barely see the stage, and you can't hear yourself clapping.

"Can you believe you're my husband?" says Casey. It's one of her clichés, an equivalent to "I love you."

"Yes," you say, but what you really mean is no. "But what I can't believe is that we're having this conversation here." You point over Casey's shoulder, where there's a shoddy wooden tower that looks like a children's playhouse. It has a spiral staircase winding up to the top, where there's a sign that reads SNIFFY THE IRISH DIVING GOAT. The two of you watch as Sniffy jaunts up to the top of the tower. He just stands there, looking too fat and glum to be diving off anything. It's hard not to laugh, and to worry that maybe you should be sadder than you are.

When you leave Sniffy's, you take a moment to sober up before driving back to the motel. The cobbled road of Beale Street is yellowed by the sunset, and most of the street performers are packing up their things. But there's one skinny boy who keeps doing back handsprings. He does them all the way down to Second Avenue, then back up to Third. You put some cash in his pail, then drive across the river. Both of you are too tired to do anything else by this time of night, so you just push the two small beds together. Casey falls asleep right away, but you keep waking up at odd hours of the night, your body slipping into the space where the two mattresses meet. Your arm is still slung over her shoulder, but you can't get rid of the sensation. You're going down, just slow enough to feel it.

You wake up early the next morning and brainstorm poetry exercises. Casey comes up with an idea she's really excited about—to have the kids write a love poem. But she's going to trick them into doing it. First, she'll tell them to write a "how to" guide to their favorite activity. It can be riding a bike, drinking a soda, reading a book. The catch is that they can't name it. They have to use their five senses. At the end, she's going to tell them to title their poem "How to Fall in Love," so the verbs of a task are transferred to an emotion.

When you arrive at the school, a few kids approach you before class, give you poems they wrote at home last night. One of them gives you a picture he drew of Sonic the Hedgehog, standing beneath the Ozarka clock tower. Already you can tell the day will go well. If students are excited, you don't have to fill that void with your own enthusiasm. You're enabled to show a range of emotion, be the insightful curmudgeon you aspire to be.

Casey's love poem goes over well, so she teaches it in every section that day. One kid writes about going to bed. "How to Fall in Love," the kid says, "You close your eyes and wait for it to happen." Another girl writes about horseback riding, yielding comical results. "How to Fall in Love," she says. "You grab his hair in your hand, then slowly bounce up and down."

By the end of the day, Casey has learned all the right things to say. Their love poems are killer. And when she gives them the title, you can tell how excited she is. "Y'all just wrote your first love poem!" she says, exaggerating her southern accent a bit, throwing her hands around in thespian gesticulations.

In the final class of the day, you notice even Benny has been quieter than normal, and that he's actually writing something, tongue protruding from the corner of his mouth in concentration.

You wait until there are no volunteers left, and then you stare vaguely toward the back of the room. "Okay, you in the back. Send us off, Benny."

He stands up, wipes his nose with his forearm, pulls his paper taught with his fingers. "I wrote mine about camping," he says.

The whole room groans.

"Quiet, everyone," you say. "It's okay if we know what the activity is. It doesn't change what the poem is about."

Benny looks around the room for a few moments, then he reads. "How to Fall in Love," he recites. "You go way out into the woods, where no one else can find you. You build a fire. Watch the stars. It's pretty uncomfortable, but you get used to it. And at the end, you have to clean up. My dad says if you do it right, it will look like you were never there to begin with."

Benny sits down, and the whole room claps for him like they did for everyone else, but something about this devastates you. It's the way Benny returns to his seat like nothing has changed. When you leave, he'll go back to being the loudest kid that everyone ignores. But something within him understands. It has all along.

When the bell rings, you say goodbye to the kids. They hand in stacks of poems. When they try to hug, you turn to the side so that they are far away from your crotch, because this is how the director has told you to hug a child—in a way that protects the bureaucracy.

On the way out of town, Casey stops at a cash-only gas station with barred windows. After paying, she stands there holding the nozzle, barefoot on dirty concrete. Turkey vultures drift above the highway that stretches across Arkansas. You don't know why, but you take the keys from the ignition and get out of the car. You think you might be having one of those moments again, when your happiness is accelerating beyond your ability to adjust. You need Casey. You want to touch her so much that you'll be able to smell her on your hands for a long time afterward.

But this is what happens instead. All the poems that were tucked into the door panel fly off in a gust of wind. The two of you chase them down, running across the parking lot and into a brown patch of grass that slopes toward a pond. It takes so long that you forget why you got out of the car in the first place, which means you never told her that you find yourself daydreaming about your past as much as you do your future. That you want to go back to the hotel room so you can reminisce about high school crushes, watch *Antiques Roadshow,* speak openly about your sexual longings, then stumble into the fluorescent bathroom, your understanding of love getting farther and farther from the examples you've been given all your life.

When you get back into the car, you put the loose poems in Casey's accordion binder, the same binder they will find in her backpack three days from now, after she goes to the library to study alone, makes a trip downstairs to go to the bathroom, then locks eyes with Eli.

"Where are the keys?" she says.

You pull them out of your pocket and hold them in your open hand.

"Were you going to drive off without me?" she jokes.

"Of course not."

You always think you're doing something else when you fall in love. You're playing basketball, talking about abortion, watching strange birds swoop into the canyons. You're losing your faith in God or driving straight into tornado alley. But what you're really doing is getting closer to someone. All it takes is a little shift in perspective.

You hand over the keys. You set the maps aside. You don't bother with your seatbelt. Because when you leave, you will leave together.

NO EXIT

ELI

SUMMER ENDS EARLY IN OZARKA this year. Just before classes begin, the atmosphere stabilizes, fog spills into groves and unkempt graveyards, and the checkered countryside turns to rust. When this happens, you think it's a sign. You wander campus pathways, passing homecoming posters, bake sales for political refugees, and giant Greek letters inlaid with gold. You hear skateboards clacking on seams of brick, professors karate chopping the air, telling entire classrooms to externalize what haunts them. It's as shifting and ugly and exciting as an amusement park. College cannot see the selfishness of its routine. It doesn't account for who it has excluded. You want to dismantle this town as if ripping a doll inside out to prove it is not alive. How this will happen, you're not sure. But you will know. You are waiting for it like a hawk in a dead tree.

Surprisingly, none of this depresses you. In fact, your mood becomes more stable once you decide there is a colossal imbalance of justice at the center of your life. You practice roundhouse kicks in Gordon's living room. You get diapers for Girlfriend and change them once a day. The two of you buy a pound of weed, and while you're waiting for it in the mail, you call your father and say you got a job, you're going to school—everything's fine. One day, you come home and Gordon is once again watching "UFO Secrets of the Third Reich" on his laptop. Technical manuals and newspaper clippings spin toward him and splat on the screen. A man in a lab coat stands before a crude matrix, outlining the principles of implosion. "Bullshit," you say. "If the Nazis had spaceships with laser guns, why didn't they use them to win the war?" Gordon laughs, and you feel proud. For a moment, you think maybe the world doesn't need to end. Maybe you just need the plan for it, and not the execution.

Then, two weeks after the semester begins, you walk into my class-room. I'm almost done taking roll when you step inside, slip across the back wall, then pull a desk to the edge of the semicircle. Your gaze ranges off to the side. You conceal your hands in your pockets. I return to the top of my roster and find the name with all the empty boxes next to it.

"Eli Habberton."

You nod.

"Welcome," I say. Then I move on. But I will remember your tensile grin, sitting there in that small anteroom of Campell Hall—the one with the broken computer they give to creative writing class-es—and how the white bricks gather behind you toward the fluo-rescent ceiling. You look good. I don't immediately think you are a malingering fuckoff, or an academic benchwarmer, or a dead man floating down a river. I assume you're taking responsibility, showing up this late. After all, whenever I come back to this scene, loss will burn you with its scalding light, and it will make you into something that, in this moment, maybe you aren't.

The reason you show up like this is because, as your life bends away from the path it was on and into the dead-end woods, you realize you can no longer afford to waste your days. No more getting high then walking down to the Ave and buying sandwiches at Bagel Mania on your credit card. No more driving down to Gold, Guns, and Guitars with Gordon, flipping through old copies of the Turner Diaries, ignoring the LOOK YES, TOUCH NO signs, then arguing with the cashier about whether or not 9/11 was an inside job. You need to soar to your death. Becoming a drug dealer will help, but you don't have the weed yet. So in the meantime, you decide to write one more story, hoping it will reveal your wounded beauty. Coming to my class simply means you will have an audience.

So for the next two weeks, you work hard and pay attention. We read a story about two druggie clerks in an emergency room who inadvertently save a guy with a hunting knife stuck in his eye. You write in a reflection paper how the plot is dominated by accidents and bad luck. Life is a series of "emergencies," you say. When I hand back your paper, I write GOOD in the margins. I tell you to speak up during class, to share your observations. But all you do is lean farther back in your chair, then flip your hair to the side with a look of superiority.

Then your first short story is due. This is your chance. You dig deep and write one called "Nameless Son." In this story, a guy arrives late to his own mother's funeral. The parking lot at the church is full, so he parks on a side street by a liquor store and a bulrush pond. When he enters, the service is already underway. The pews are crowded with unfamiliar people. He finds a folding chair and sits in the back, but he can't hear the pastor through his crackling microphone and rhotic accent. He thinks he hears the pastor say, "Never trust the good times." But he's not sure. Eventually, everyone raises their hands and walks toward the casket like they're at a concert. He can't see. He can't get through. The story ends.

If I were to read this, I'd tell you it's a great start. "It's Kafkaesque," I might say. And maybe I'd ask what inspired you to write it, leading to a heart-to-heart about your mother's death. But this is not what happens. In one of your typical acts of self-abnegation, you throw this story away. You decide it is too personal, lacks grandiosity. But since your story is due in three days, you go on a weed binge and write a new one called "Dead Girl." It's about a pharmaceutical salesman in New York who wants to kill his vain girlfriend so he can love her. It reads like a bad mashup of *American Psycho* and *Friends*. As in, it's macabre and anti-establishment in all the obvious ways, yet everyone has nice apartments and endless amounts of free time. In the final scene, the narrator grabs a kitchen knife and stabs his girlfriend with several piston-like motions, but she doesn't die. So he jumps out a window onto Park Avenue (though he's supposed to be in Greenwich—you've never been to New York). On the way down he screams, "We're all furious fucking dreamers!"

After reading this story, I send you an email, asking if you could meet me in my office to discuss your work. And let me be honest. I don't do this to figure out what comic alternate reality you are living in, or to shove a bottle of Risperidone down your throat, or to fill out a Structured Assessment of Violence Risk in Youth worksheet. In fact, your story doesn't alarm me in any way. This semester, for example, has already been the semester of backyard pool suicides. Before that, the semester of old men "rescuing" strippers with their love. And before that, the "I blame Lolita" semester. Besides, I'm the one who tells students that love is acceptance in the face of "All this information" (opening my arms, as if gesturing to the world). I say that everyone is an iceberg, that all their weight and mass and meaning is below the surface. Eli, I wasn't worried about you. I called you to my office because your story struck me as rushed and illogical. I was just worried you missed too much class, that you needed special attention for your writing to improve. And maybe I should have been alarmed, but for a figure to be perceived, it needs to stand out from its background.

This semester, all the English faculty offices were relocated to a converted apartment complex at the edge of campus between a junkyard of university vehicles and a gravel escarpment. The stairway outside is pulling away from the building, and we have to bring our own toilet paper and light bulbs if we want to shit or see. In other words, my conference attendance has been shoddy, and I doubt you'll show up—but you do.

"Dr. Bressinger?" you say, standing at my door. It's cold outside, but you're wearing a T-shirt and jeans, hands cupping your armpits.

"Glad you made it."

"Barely." You sit down, manage an affable sigh. But then you seem nervous. You blink rapidly, sit on the edge of the chair. So I push your story aside and ask about your life. You're from Earl Heights. You missed two weeks of school due to a family emergency. You want to be a writer. And when I ask if you have a job, you tell me you're an intern at a farm in Pulaski. When I ask what you do for them, you say: "I don't know—pick up rocks, mainly." A lie I will never understand.

When there's a lull, I motion to your story. "This," I say. "I like how this was strange and surprising. But I wanted to talk to you because there's a lot to unpack."

"I know," you say, your voice oddly insubstantial. "Like how the search for happiness is filled with pain."

And that's when I see it, whatever it is, like a bird passing in front of the moon. "What do you mean?"

For some time, you stare at the wall, and I think you may be tracing a feeling to its origin.

"Eli?"

You nod. It's afternoon, and the quality of light in my office is good. I can see into your eyes. Free-floating, marred by red.

"What about the main character," I say. "From the beginning of the story, he's angry. Where does that anger come from?"

"I don't know. He's just angry." You lean back into your cockeyed chair.

"Okay—well, I want you to consider two things." First, I explain how it's problematic to write a story in order to prove a point. How what can be evoked cannot be described and vice versa. Second, I tell you the most dislikable characters deserve our empathy and respect.

"That's the thing," you say. "I am being sincere. He's a terrible person."

I cross my legs and arms, try to make myself as small as possible before I say something critical. "Readers should determine that on their own," I say. "But you? The writer? Your job is to love your characters, to know them like you know yourself. Hate has this way of refusing to accumulate more knowledge."

It's one of my favorite pieces of advice, one that most writing teachers repeat to infinity. But for many years, I will picture what you saw when you watched me say this. And each time I do, I will see a smug professor who thinks he has all the answers, whose search for empathy is also a desire for control, whose constant lecturing has turned his mouth into a door that swings open so freely it has lost its function.

But for the moment, you let me believe I've been helpful.

"I understand," you say. "I think I can write a better story."

"That's good. Do you have any questions?"

You stand up, look at the room like it has been stripped of its geography. "Thanks," you say. "I have really enjoyed this class."

All this happens on a Friday. After you leave, I step out into the languor of the evening, where the sun dims to the color of tarnished brass, and a girl in a jester costume skips through campus as she does at the end of every week. When I get home, Eddie is on my porch. He's wearing that houndstooth sport coat he bought from Goodwill. He looks coldcocked. So we go down to Tailspin Tavern and run the pool table all night. He talks about Casey, describing love like it's a cliff he's walking toward. When the bar closes, we go back to my place. We say goodnight. Before I fall asleep, I tell myself that I've logged another adequate day.

Meanwhile, a small part of me is gone. It is with you now. It's there as you walk home from my office, past the globed streetlights, the dewy evening windows, through cold air that's cut with wood smoke. You're muttering, punching your fists toward the sidewalk, because your story was supposed to release you from pain. It was supposed to explain how love is a sheen that can't be cast over everything, not like people think it can. But after talking to me, you've tumbled down into a familiar pit, where all that can be confirmed is how little other people understand about you. Your life stands alone in its unbearable uniqueness. So you decide to give up on writing. This makes you feel better, even though giving up has always felt like failure. The difference now is that the end is coming, which means the worse things get, the closer you are to reaching the border of your darkness. And the more you abandon, the more lies you tell, the more you will be inured to failure, and whatever you choose to leave behind will require nothing from you. It will have to explain itself.

A few days later, you come home to Gordon standing in the living room. He turns to you sharply. This is unusual because, if he's not in class or at work, he's usually behind a cloud of weed smoke, long blond hair spilling out from a dirty Pikachu beanie, playing *Black Ops 2* and listening to Frank Sinatra.

"It's gone," he says.

You wait for him to elaborate, but when he doesn't, your eyes start to wander around the room.

"The weed," he says. "It was at a FedEx in Rueben for a week. Now the tracking number is invalid."

For a moment, the disaster of losing $2,000 worth of product hits you, especially the fact that you were going to sell it and pay for rent, food, and tuition. But then you remember how everything is supposed to be going wrong.

"Relax," you say. "It's probably just sitting in Rueben. Unless your guy at the mail room is up to something."

"Not possible. We can trust Caesar."

"His name is *Caesar*?" you say, startling Girlfriend, who gets up from her bed, just a sock drawer that sits on the floor next to the couch.

Gordon shrugs. He leans down to pet Girlfriend but she clucks into the kitchen. "We shouldn't have done this," he says.

"I think we should go to FedEx and talk to someone in person."

"Are you joking?" Gordon says. "The package was probably seized. Can Bitcoin data be traced? I need to incinerate my computer. The police are probably across the street with a shotgun mic right now." Gordon paces the living room as he says all this, waving his arms like a drunken semaphore.

But you pretend not to hear him. You take your keys out of your pocket, leaving the door open as you step outside and into your car. The sun shines after a downpour, and all the bare, wayward branches glimmer with liquid. You pick a radio station. You put the car in reverse, and eventually Gordon emerges, a flat-billed baseball cap pulled down over his eyes.

Rueben is a regional tourist city in southern Missouri. It's the self-proclaimed "Wax Museum Capital of the World" and is known for its Confederate heritage tours, Dolly Parton–themed restaurants, and an airport shaped like a log cabin, which is filled with taxidermied animals and a decorative water wheel. To get there, you drive two hours northeast out of Ozarka, past small towns that begin and end with cemeteries, through aisles of fallow farmland. You know you're close when the freeway expands and you start seeing billboards for tiger sanctuaries, family folk bands, and a comedian named Kirby Crawford who does every show in a propeller hat and overalls.

The FedEx is in a giant parking lot next to Liquor World. Gordon says he wants to stay in the car, so you walk into the building alone. Inside, there are no customers, just employees futzing with a copy machine and ziggurats of packages.

"Can I help you?" says a short man behind the counter.

"Yes, I'm missing one of my parcels," you say, handing him the paper with the tracking number on it. You feel like you're moving in slow motion.

"Let's see," he says, swiftly poking the keyboard. He repeats this action several times. "Hold on." He disappears into a back room.

While you wait, you watch behind the counter. A tall guy with uneven hair and a black eye keeps walking over to his manager and saying, "Should we release the hounds on this one?"

The small guy comes out of the back room, empty handed. "I have no record of this," he says. "You should contact the sender."

You laugh involuntarily, because it's not like you can just call up the Silk Road. And when you stop laughing, the man sways back and forth, like some fog has appeared between you and he's trying to look through it. You find it amazing, how misfortune is starting to give your life structure and meaning. So what if bad things happen? You are free to make them worse.

"Sir?" the guy says, finally.

"Thanks for your help."

Back in the car, you tell Gordon and he shakes his head, starts biting his fingernails. It all seems so petty and unimaginative. But Gordon is still your friend. His pain is still partially yours. So instead of driving straight home, you take a detour to the entertainment district, hoping to find a casino or strip club or some other attraction that will change the mood. All you find are white ladies gathered around tour buses, marquees advertising washed-up country singers, and a piano bar that only plays Billy Joel songs from the nineties. When the strip ends and morphs into car dealerships, you turn into a place called Pizza Pals.

You buy dinner, ask Gordon questions, hoping he will launch into a rant about the Illuminati or how pop stars are ruled by the queen of the lizard people. But you can't get through to him. He tears up paper napkins and piles them into a heap, while in the background, a large animatronic mouse lip syncs "End of the Line" by the Traveling Wilburys.

It isn't until you are back in the car, driving toward the impending moon, that Gordon finally says something. "Is everything all right with you?"

"Sure—I'm totally fine."

Gordon leans toward you and stares, like he's looking for some drama that's supposed to be inherent in your face, but he can't find it. "Do you remember when we first met and you told me about your mom? You weren't totally fine then. Whatever happened with that?"

"You mean, am I still sad that my mom is dead?"

"Jesus Christ—no. You said you were like, losing sight of who you were."

At first, you don't respond. You stare into the light that is bowing out of the sky. You drive through places like Needmore, Beeftown, Whitehaven.

"You know what I've realized?" you say eventually. "That it's impossible to forget who you are. We spend our entire lives turning into one person—that's it."

Gordon starts to speak, but you interrupt him. "And about what I said last summer. Sure, every once in a while I feel weird, like a pane of glass or something is separating me from the world. Like I'm locked out of my own life. But it doesn't last for very long."

"Okay," Gordon says. "I've been wondering about that."

Out here, there are no streetlights. You can't see the sad cafés or shotgun houses or defunct post offices because your headlights barely reach beyond the perimeter of the road, where white crosses lean on guardrails and small animals swoon in the grass.

"Anyways," says Gordon. "Thanks for driving all the way out here." He leans over and turns on the radio, flipping through religious hollering and Mexican folk.

You can't drive at night on roads like this without picturing a semi truck around every corner, parked halfway in your lane, its white rear door waiting to appear like a sudden blank page. So you slow down. You hold your breath like you're moving through a tunnel. It gets so quiet you start to feel like you're waiting for something to plow through the swaggering trees, enter the car, and ring like you're inside a giant bell. But it doesn't come. That's fine. You have waited long enough to see clearly on your own, without anyone's help, to know that all you have to do is cling to the belly of the road you are already on. Keep missing all of your exits, one by one.

Two weeks later, a graduate student studying applied physics at UC Berkeley climbs to the top of a lifeguard tower with an AR-15 and shoots into a crowded beach. Among the people he kills are an eight-year-old boy, a volleyball coach, and a Lebanese journalist who recently emigrated after her family died in a car bomb. The shooter's name is Taylor Blake, and when the police show up and return fire, he tries to take his own life, but holds the gun at such an angle that he doesn't die but lobotomizes himself. He's breathing when they find him, and his eyes are open, staring impassively at the sky.

For the next few days, Taylor Blake is everywhere. On the news, you watch as the authorities search his apartment for abnormalities, finding a notebook filled with clownish poems and misquoted lines from French philosophers. You read headlines like GUNMAN IS LONER SCHIZO WHO FELT NO PAIN scrolling across the television. Family members are interviewed. The president gives a speech and cries a little. The price of ammunition spikes. But ultimately, what you take away from all this is how suddenly important this man has become. His name is on the tip of everyone's tongue. Sure, these murders are unjustified and impish and illogical, but he has shown everyone what a lark their lives are, and in doing so has disambiguated his own. You watch as all the insults and legal actions and think pieces written about him express the same underlying point. He has abandoned the world, and the world—wanting to overpower him—has unwittingly elevated him instead.

But everyone has heard this story before, which means it only changes the world for a moment, the same way that snow falling at night can be gone in the morning. During this time, you compare yourself to Taylor Blake and all the seemingly homogenous assholes that came before him, but what you are going through seems bigger and different and more inexplicable. You believe you are fated for a different end, and in this way Taylor Blake seems more like a small town that you would have missed had you blinked while driving through it.

Meanwhile, Gordon tells you he's going to focus on school and his job at the restaurant. You start seeing him less, then at one point he disappears for three days, and when he comes back he's with a guy you've never seen before. Together they walk down to the rainwater creek in the backyard, gather jagged chunks of shale, and make a fire pit in a clearing of bald swamp maples. Within the pit, they arrange broken furniture and appliances from Gordon's junk pile, douse it with lighter fluid, and talk indistinctly beside the blaze. Eventually, Gordon comes inside to grab his whisky and invites you to hang out, but it already feels like you have been excluded. So you stay. You fall asleep listening to their muffled voices, then awaken when you hear footsteps at the edge of a dream. No one is there, but contours of bootdirt lead to the fridge and back outside.

You put on your shoes and walk out to the fire. Gordon introduces you to the guy, whose name is Dave, and you can't decide whether they know each other from work or school. On one hand, Dave has a narrow, moose-like beard and walks with a cane. On the other, he has the kind of chubby muscles endemic to meal plans and university rec centers, and he's wearing a tight GO COONS T-shirt (a phrase OU recently banned, which only increased its popularity among people who fetishize racist dog whistles). While you puzzle through this, he throws a broken tricycle on top of the fire, the flames licking the sky above your head. Within the blaze, you can see a cardboard poster of a giant panda and fence wood that you once helped Gordon steal from a fraternity's utility shed.

Dave backs away from the fire, swatting the burning particles in the air. "By the way," he says, "what's up with that chicken I seen in there?"

You look at Gordon, but he just nods at you. "It's a chicken," you say.

"But it's a pet, though—isn't it?" He asks the question like he's uninterested in getting an answer.

You start explaining Girlfriend's story, how you took her from that jobsite in Aloma and showed up at Gordon's house. While you talk, Dave sits down on a bucket. He takes a knife out of his pocket, cuts the top off an empty beer can, then spits chew into it.

"How 'bout that now," he says when your story ends. He doesn't look at you, just stares into the fire with a flinty expression.

"By the way," you mock, "what's up with your leg?"

He shifts his weight on the bucket. "Combine harvester."

"That's too bad," you say, responding so quickly that you cut off his last syllable. You grab a rusted tire iron, start splintering pieces off a futon frame. No one says anything.

The three of you pace the flame in silence until it dims and the darkness erases all the corners out of the sky. It's cold, and when you move closer to the warmth, Gordon starts describing a reality show about people who have a fetish for ghost sex. He recounts a woman who dresses up in a sexy negligee and waits to be ravaged by the condensation on her window. This is one of his typical conversational tropes, but now he speaks with an odd wariness, hoping to change the mood. This makes you feel bad, so you stop trying to outdo Dave with your alpha male scorn. You laugh, and surprisingly this makes you feel more powerful. So you laugh harder, and when you look at Dave, he seems tethered to nothing, like a wavy face in a dark pool of water.

What you have come to realize is that yielding to the remaining days of your life is not a weakness, but a private weapon. It is why, in these final months, you smile as if gazing into a brighter future. You drive to Earl Heights and help your father demolish a living room. You lift weights. You floss your teeth. You surf the Internet and watch videos of people falling over, men playing pranks on their hot wives, fatal altercations with law enforcement. Sometimes you say "Namaste" instead of "Hello." You have found that this kind of behavior is advantageous because no one can suspect or challenge you. They don't know that you are looking at them and wondering why they are so engaged by this life and convinced that it is saturated with meaning. They don't know that you are waiting for the moment that will unravel everything.

Weeks later, you agree to go to a Halloween party with Gordon and Dave. At first you're apprehensive, but then you dig through Gordon's stuff and find a black rain slicker and a grotesque latex pig mask. You put it on and look in the mirror and feel an instant confidence. The psychotic black hair glued between its ears and the cubist expression on its face—puffed cheeks, gloopy eyes, wrinkled lips— makes it seem like there is nothing out there, on your moral horizon. You walk out into the living room and find Gordon, who is dressed up as Baby Jaxx, a child actor turned pop star who wears intricate top buns and mascara so heavy it looks like a bandit's mask. He is standing on the couch, pantomiming a live performance of her hit song, a rhythmic dance number about a stripper with a heart of gold.

After Dave shows up, the three of you walk across town toward Raccoon Road, which is a street behind the football stadium where noise ordinances have been written out of city code. Dave isn't wearing a costume, and you can't tell if he's embarrassed or excited by Gordon's mini skirt and crop top. He keeps slapping Gordon's ass and laughing. "You're a sexy little bitch," he says, while Gordon conceals a discomfort that's not purely physical.

The party house is a wood-paneled rambler with a dirt yard that looks like it floods every time it rains. Before entering, you put on the mask, and the tiny rectangular eyeholes are more disorienting than you expected. You can't really look up or down. It's like you're staring at the world behind a wall with two jagged peepholes. You only catch glimpses of things. Refrigerator. Spilled candy. Tibetan prayer flags. A girl in a bikini wearing a Chewbacca mask. Various cat ears and war bonnets. People ask about your costume and give you looks, but they don't seem to expect a response. You feel godlike and featureless. So you just snort, loudly and aggressively, like a hog protecting food. You lose track of Gordon and Dave, end up standing by a defunct fireplace with some strangers.

"We've been voting on sexiest outfits so far," says a girl who you think is dressed up as a unicorn. "So far, you're winning."

You look at her closer, regard the glitter on her face, the horn affixed to her head, and the pink prom dress revealing what look like Bible verses tattooed on her shoulder. You don't respond with words. You get in her face and snort loudly, and she shrieks in delight.

"Yeah man," says a guy standing beside her, wearing a cheap lab coat and a plastic stethoscope. "No one dresses up as anything scary anymore."

"Listen," the unicorn says. "What is your astrological sign?"

You tilt your head.

"Gemini—I knew it!"

Just then, the loud roar of a distorted guitar rings throughout the house, which cuts your conversation short. A band called Lap-Dog has set up in the den. They're an aggressive surf-rock band that headline OzarkaStock every year. The lead singer is six feet tall, has armpit hair dyed electric blue, and often sucks on the microphone in between her shouty vocals. People start pushing you, so you push back. By the fifth song, you're tired and sweat is dripping out of the bottom of your mask. You pace the house looking for Gordon, but you can't find him. Eventually you're in the backyard and see the unicorn girl, who is smoking a cigarette at the edge of the fence.

"You again," she says.

You nod.

"You haven't said anything all night, have you? That's dedication." She flicks her half-smoked cigarette over the fence into the neighbor's yard.

It's that part of the night when everyone's costumes are coming apart. People are genuflecting in the grass for no reason. They are screaming the Ozarka Raccoon cheer and quitting halfway.

"This may sound crazy," she says, "but I've probably learned more about you at this party than anyone else, and you haven't even said a word."

You nod.

"But that's a college party for you, huh?"

She stands there for a second, stoop-shouldered in the cold, looking at you like she sees self-assurance and skill, like she wants to experience the darkness you live inside. And for a second, you entertain the idea of falling in love. You fantasize that she tries to save you, but you can't love her back because love obligates you to take care of yourself. "I stopped caring about myself a long time ago," you say, and it stings her heart in a way that it has never been stung before.

So, in one of your typical combinations of grandiosity and ineptitude, you take off your mask. You grab her hand, then you lean toward her for a kiss, but it is a kiss that does not understand its destination.

"Ahh," she says, turning her face away from you. "I wasn't expecting that."

You interpret this as an invitation to retry, so you pull her close again, but she scrunches her face toward its center and shakes her head. "Stop!" she says. She tries to pull away but your hand is clasped around her wrist. You're standing still and she's pulling away, and it almost looks like she is trying to lead you somewhere. Eventually, you let go, which causes her to tumble to the ground.

That's when you pick up your mask. You don't say anything, just put it back on with both hands, not realizing that it looks like you're part of some decapitation myth. The girl is gone by the time you align your eyes with the holes. You consider chasing after her, but the comfort and anonymity that the mask affords is no longer there.

So you leave through the side fence and spend the rest of the night wandering around town. You walk down to Huntsville Road, past all the distribution warehouses and atrophied barns. You cross the freeway. You find a reservoir you've never seen before, where the stars reflect in the black and superterrestrial water. Eventually, you walk down MLK, past all the discount grocery stores, the parking lots scattered with fertilized trees, and end up at a Brenda's Burger. The lobby is closed, so you use to the intercom at the drive-thru.

"I'd like a double big-n-spicy," you say.

"Sir, I can't serve you unless you are in a vehicle."

"Really? I walked all the way down here."

"Sir," she says again, reproachfully.

You sigh angrily, implementing the stereotype of a mistreated customer, then roll back on your heels.

"Bitch."

The speaker crackles. "What?"

"I was saying you have a really nice voice—why are you working a crappy job like this?"

"Well, it's a job."

"What's your name?"

"Sarah."

"Sarah," you say, then repeat it with a somewhat mocking tone. "Sar-ah. If I could give you one piece of advice, it would be to leave town for a while. You won't want to be here when it happens."

"What?" she asks, but you're already gone. Something about the night feels complete—as if telling someone about your plan has created a deeper code that you now have to live by, as if your anger now has a clearer object. So you go home and sleep so soundly that when you wake up, you feel as if you've aged several years. You remember Dave, Gordon, and the girl you tried to kiss as if from a long time ago, and you feel embarrassed and sorry for them. After all, they don't realize that you can't be their friend. To do so would be to travel back into the badlands of the life you are leaving behind.

From now on, you feel as if you are occupying a secondary universe. The meaning of the everyday world has changed. You stop and listen to jeans tumbling in the dryer because you are waiting for instruction. You watch the sunlight shake through the trees because you realize, for the first time in your life, that the word sunset is just a manner of speaking—it's just out there, floating. Every action is a sane behavior in service of this empowering mirage. The way you tell Gordon you'll be moving into your own place the end of the semester. The TV dinners you load into the freezer. The way you agree to see *The Nutcracker* with your father and Joe at the Don Butler Arts Center, wearing your best sun-bleached work shirt, and at the end pushing aside all your lamentations about your ersatz family in order to tell your father you are happy that he found someone to spend his life with. You almost lament the life you are exiting, but when your father says he loves you, all you can think is how foolish it is, since at this point he has no idea who you actually are.

It's around this time that you reach into a pile of dirty clothes and inadvertently grab the cold muzzle of Gordon's rifle. You haven't seen it for months, and now that you are looking at it again, it seems to carry new meaning. So you take it into Gordon's room and point it at yourself in the greasy mirror that hangs on the back of the door, expecting to feel similar to how you did when you were wearing the pig mask—but something is off. The rifle is a Chinese-type SKS with a wooden stock and a ten-round magazine. It doesn't look like you are harnessing power that wants to be used. Instead, it looks like you should be hunting varmints. Later, you go online and watch videos of the type of people who own this gun. They are old men in basements with unreconstructed accents. The most common topic is how cheap the gun is and how it's good for hunting in the rain because you don't want to drag your nice rifle through the mud. And yet, they still turn it over in their hands as if examining a jewel. They stroll out into unkempt woods to shoot at targets and old refrigerators. Songs like "Crazy Train" and "Down with the Sickness" fill the silence between gunshots.

One of the last videos you watch is a guy who demonstrates how to field strip the gun. He modifies it with a new folding stock, pistol grip, and a thirty-round magazine. Now, the gun looks black and tactical. He carries the gun and camera out to a long field of dead sage grass that's yellowed with morning sun, rides an ATV to one end of it, and sets up an entire box of crackers on top of a fence. Then, in one fastidious motion, he unloads the entire magazine as the crackers explode in the distance. When he's done, crows swoop down out of the sky as if on command.

You find the same modifications online, but when they come in the mail, they don't have instructions. First you can't get the trigger mechanism to pop out, and once you do, your hands and the kitchen table are smeared with Cosmoline. Then the wooden stock won't slide off. You look for a hammer but all you find is an ice pick that's part of Gordon's knife set and a brick you can use to smash the other end. The sun traces an arc through the window. Eventually, you find a lever in front of the magazine that needs to be flicked, and the modifications are finished. You bring it back to the mirror in

Gordon's room, and now when you point it at yourself, you strike a baleful glare. You raise the gun above your head, the way you might hold something up to the light in order to see through it.

The front door swings open. Keys sliding across the coffee table. Gordon is on the phone. He opens his bedroom door, then stops at the threshold and looks at you.

"Whoa," he says.

When the bullet goes through Gordon's chest and shatters his sternum, it seems to impart a tremendous amount of kinetic energy into his body, but by the time his back slams against the wall, that kinetic energy is gone, and his body folds up on itself like cardboard.

You stand there looking at him for a second. You feel bad that your friend is dead, but you don't feel responsible for it. The fact that you have taken his life means it was always yours to begin with.

What you do next feels like it happens before you decide to do it. This makes you think that there is some preordained, fixed destiny you are fulfilling, when in reality it has just been retold to you so many times that there seems to be no original model after which you are patterned. It's like a riot that no one remembers starting, but it doesn't take much to grab a rock, to take aim at a building already set on fire.

You open Gordon's closet, grab his camouflage camping backpack, fold the stock of the gun against the chamber, and slip it inside. And when you walk out to your car, a neighbor is peeking out his window, and sees what he will later describe as a completely unguarded expression on your face. Week-old snow is still piled on shady patches of grass, and puddles are icing over again in the absence of the sun. Without hesitation, you drive up Arkansas Avenue, past the neoclassical buildings with multi-pitched roofs. You park in the fire lane next to a corridor on the north side of campus.

It's near the end of finals week, which means campus is filled with students studying in abnormal places. They are sitting in lobbies, up against glass windows, reading on treadmills, beneath potted plants in administration buildings. Others are emerging from their dorms, rolling their suitcases through icy puddles, half jogging toward cars waiting at the bottom of hills.

The library was remodeled a few years ago by an architect who slapped a glass box on the front of the sandstone façade. Inside it hosts large ergonomic furniture, tranquil paintings, and accent walls painted in bold colors. Something about it feels constantly diurnal. Your boots clomp on the flagstone floors through the quiet, past the rows of workstations, the students scrolling through Word documents, cross-legged and shoeless, surrounded by paper coffee cups and half-eaten teriyaki bowls. They are defining price-gouging, punching calculators, writing "strictly within the framework of" in the middle of every clause. When you get to the other end of the Learning Commons, you slip into a tiny hallway that leads to an exit stairwell. You unstrap your backpack, set it on the floor, and take out the gun. You are making sure the magazine is loaded and the safety is off when you hear footsteps echoing off the walls.

The person coming down the stairs is Casey, carrying a binder filled with graded papers. There's a red toothbrush in her cardigan pocket. For years afterward, the existence of this one small item will be a source of unrest for Eddie, because carrying a toothbrush around was never—as far as he knew—one of her eccentricities. Why did she have it? Where had she been, and where did she think she was going?

When she rounds the last railing, she sees you there pointing the rifle at her. She doesn't have time to recognize what is happening. She doesn't scream or move. She just looks at you, and then she's gone.

When you emerge from the stairwell, most everyone is already looking in your direction, but something about the comfort of their life briefly lags into this moment. Because of this, the first few kids basically watch themselves get shot. They don't look particularly jolted, just oddly circumspect, like they walked through the door scanner and set off the alarm, though they weren't carrying any books. Eventually, the moment catches up to itself, and when the students and librarians run to the door, that's when you start firing with blank resolution.

I suppose I could explain how unreal the world looks to someone who refuses to see its future. How you hardly believe in the lives you are blighting, and therefore do not envision all the lungs that will be pumped with ambu bags, the emergency thoracotomies, the kids who will wake up and whose nerve damage will force them to relearn how to blink or smile. You don't realize how no one here will go bowling or shoot off fireworks for years afterward. You can't picture how the buses will arrive at the fairground with evacuated students. How people will wake up after surgery and feel the bullets still inside them, waiting to tear through. The hearing loss and tunnel vision. The garbage cans that will be emptied on your father's porch. The pathological bereavements. The unfamiliar selves waiting on the other side. How many casseroles will be made, how many friends will pick up the phone to call someone for support, only to realize the person they are calling is gone. You can't see all the votaried windows. How the red geraniums in front of our houses will no longer just be red geraniums, but ones that exist in a new world, where even a color carries with it a memory of pain.

But there is a future you are imagining, and it begins when all the cameras, counselors, and outraged analysts show up and start plugging away at the narrative into which you know you'll fit—the one that will regard you as an aberration. That will search for your manifesto. That will say you don't *look* like a murderer. It is the one that largely ignores a drive-by shooter who kills seven people at a Laundromat in Atlantic City, but will talk like you are some mystical creature, some evil that has nothing to do with the cultural malfunctions you flew into like a bird toward an invisible window. In other words, you know as well as anyone that your life and the ground you walk on has already been made sacred. You have already been given this final opportunity to access your privilege. All you're doing is showing up to take it.

When the chamber is empty, there are bodies on the floor in parts of the room you don't remember shooting. Broken glass is still falling and ringing like wind chimes in a storm. You take a step forward, and that's when you feel something grabbing your leg.

"Stop," a voice says. You look down and a girl is hiding under a Formica table, holding onto your ankle. But there's an entire reality separating the two of you. She is speaking to you from the unknown country of your dreams.

You drop the gun and walk out the back door to a campus that is empty. The trees shift in the silence. Birds are flying upside down and backward. You get in your car, re-enter traffic. You make it all the way down to College Avenue, past Ozarka Cleaners, DressBarn, Discount Chicken Company, Andy's Frozen Custard, Mattress Outlet, ShoeCarnival. And when you crest a hill there is an almost sinister openness to the sky—not so much like you are escaping to somewhere in particular, but like the whole world is falling backward and erasing itself behind you.

EVERYTHING LOST COMES BACK AGAIN

EDDIE

Alone in my living room, you are putting on a sweatshirt you will never wear again. It is teal, chewed up around the neck, with a cartoon sailboat sewn across the chest. You already dug out your baggy, decade-old running pants from the suitcases piled against my couch. It has been an hour since the university announced there is an active shooter on campus, and you can't get hold of Casey. You've called, texted, emailed. Your only option is to run two miles home and hope she answers the door in her pajamas.

So you sprint down College Avenue, where people stare at you from the window booths of Waffle House, from under raccoon-themed Christmas Lights, wearing cowboy boots and statement necklaces, thronged in the frigid air without coats. You do not care how desperate you look, sprinting through the half-halted ceremony of a Friday night, past Shotz, Don's Eat Place, Tailspin Tavern. How the sweat on your beard is turning to ice and the thinning hair on your head is slicked up in a sort of middle-aged mohawk. Soon you reach the part of town that's all law offices, steepled churches with gigantic rec centers, wide vistas of asphalt parking lots. It's so quiet you can hear your staccato breathing. Streetlights spin your shadow around on the pavement like the hand of a clock.

By the time you reach the base of Mount Palmer, you've convinced yourself Casey is dead. Such an assumption allows you to withdraw from the present and inhabit the future, where she will have been dead a long time. You have already endured your own obsessive nostalgias and hormonal cascades. You have waited in line at the campus Wal-Mart pharmacy for your beta blockers. You have dented the blank face of my freezer with your fists. You have wandered into the pitch black of an ice storm. Enduring all this will feel like getting soaked by death and never drying off completely, but in time you will learn how to cope. You will wake up in the morning and drink coffee in our small kitchen. You will organize poetry explications in a neat stack, put a wool hat on your bald head and go to class, where you will tell your college freshman that the point of literature is to imagine a future beyond the reality that is rendering before them. Then, while they complete an in-class writing exercise, you will look beyond the rows of bleached hair and photorealistic camo jackets and entertain a maladaptive daydream—what life would have been several months after Casey was killed, the two of you navigating the new reality of her pregnancy. "Don't you ever get sad you'll never experience childbirth?" you write in your notebook, since you are brainstorming for a dialogue exercise. After so many years, you still participate in any assignment you give your students.

Eventually, the day will end. You will walk back to our house—because, in this future, we will be roommates—and after you crawl into bed and start reading, I will walk by and pause in your doorway. I will hump my laundry basket and stick out my tongue. You will not see me. On my way back from the laundry room, I will do it again, this time with hand gestures. You will smile and put down your book. Goodnight, Steven, you will say, and then you will close your door, creep back into bed, pull down your boxers, and grab hold of yourself. The sheets will whisper against your hand. You will go back to that old house on Reagan Avenue, focusing on small things to recreate the scene. It's summer, the AC unit whirrs. Some band down at the coffee shop playing their daddy-take-me-back-to-Jesus music. The damaged wood floor takes shape beneath your feet, and the perforated lamp Casey had in the dorms spreads misshapen stars onto the ceiling. Then Casey is on the bed. She is undressing. She is sitting straight-backed on the edge like George Washington. You will start stroking yourself, close off the scene until it is just the two of you, at a point in your past when everything is woven together and paused.

The point of all of this is that now, at the base of the mountain, running alongside overgrown culverts in the dark, you are learning how to soften the blow before it lands. You are imagining the life that sorrow will build instead of the sorrow itself.

Eventually, you arrive at the house you moved into a year ago, the one with mulberry trees out front that stain the sidewalk a firework red. There are two front doors leading into a vast-ceilinged living room and kitchen. When you clean the rafters, it only takes two weeks for cobwebs to appear again. A near-vertical ladder/staircase leads to the bedroom in the attic. When you will remember how everything went wrong, you will remember it taking place here. How it felt to fuck someone who doubted you. Where you learned the hard way that, if you punish someone for feeling caged in, you can only expect them to view you as the thing that has caged them.

You step inside. You call her name. While you wait, your eyes adjust, and the patterns of the empty room grow out of the darkness. Textured archway. Satin trim. Gnarled houseplant. Antlers dangling with jewelry. It seems even emptier with the lights on. You climb upstairs and rip the sheets off the unoccupied bed. In the bathroom, you tear down the shower curtain. You're so out of your mind you look for her in closets and under couch cushions, throw a loaded dish rack against the wall, run several laps around the house in mud that tries to suck the shoes off your feet. Then back inside, you tear the house apart again looking for her backpack, then her laptop, then her accordion binder. All of these are gone, which means Casey went to the library. She gets more work done in the panopticon of the reading room. She likes to feel as if she's being watched.

From now on, your body will remember what is happening in ways that your conscious mind will not. As you run back toward campus, the adrenaline fueling you is creating deep neurological patterns in your brain. Everything lost will come back to this moment. It is why, in a sense, you will always be running. It is why, months later, you will fall asleep and wake up in your underwear outside Waffle House, on the bike trail, in the strange corridors of the brick buildings behind my house. On the slow walk back, chest heaving, you will habitually look over your shoulder. You will flinch at the sound of footsteps, look into the windows of parked cars, reach into your pocket for the ringing phone that isn't there. You will do all of this because there is one fragment of an idea that will always be embedded in your mind—the chance that Casey is simply looking for you at the same time you are looking for her, that both of you are running to the same places over and over again, just taking different paths to get there.

IN ABSENTIA

ROSE

WHEN FRESHMAN YEAR ENDS, YOU decide to spend the summer in Ozarka. You rent a cheap studio, fill it with pictures, food, and thrift store furniture. You read books at the community pool attached to Ellen's apartment complex. You get a job at a grocery store in the historic part of town, where Osage trees litter the street with their bumpy fruit. On your walks home, you take the scenic route. You pass old homes with gardens of christflowers, vintage lamps brightening living rooms like giant fish tanks. Families eat in dining rooms. Televisions buzz with bland sitcoms. You fantasize that one day, you'll find yourself in a house like this (though recently you've resisted this daydream, telling yourself to stop grasping for some fake middle-class life vest). But now, you've decided it's safe enough to let your guard down. You're starting to think about yourself like a plant that simply grows into the light, whenever there is some.

It's around this time you drive with Ellen to a one-story hospital in a town called Cairo, smelling the sulfuric odor of industrial cow lots, watching the evening clouds drain out of the sky. When you check in at the front desk, a midwife named Deborah intercepts you.

"Just wanted to give you a heads up," she says. "I think you'll be taking pictures of his feet, mainly." Her eyes are hypervigilant, assessing you from beyond eyeglasses studded with rhinestones at each corner.

"Thanks," says Ellen. "It will be okay—we've been doing this a while."

"I just never know what type of volunteers they are going to send me."

You used to be nervous, carrying photography equipment down the shadowless halls of hospitals, past photographs of highland forests, nurses in aqua scrubs, empty wheelchairs. You would pause before walking into suites with their tiny sinks, rolling stools, and examination tables. You would try to think of something to say, but every word was its own quagmire. You kept imagining the happy narrative script these babies were supposed to be born into, and how instead their lives are a fault and an embarrassment and a source of nameless dread.

But this was before you realized you weren't exactly mourning the child by feeling this way. You were mourning your own illusions of happy and unmarred pregnancies. And once you realized this, you began noticing how many of these women are more prepared than you thought. They aren't alone, with phlegmatic nurses and husbands in corners. They have midwives, postpartum doulas. They know our infant mortality rate (a "national embarrassment," as Ellen puts it). Some have already considered if they want to get pregnant again, and if they'd be able to give things to their new baby that were intended for their deceased child. Realizing this allows you to spare them your pity. And in place of saying "I'm so sorry for your loss," you can fetch them a bagel, joke about exam gowns shaped like paper lanterns, listen to how Demerol caused them to hallucinate about the nurse tending to a roaring fire. In doing so, you're able to show them that you, too, live in a world where life can get better after an unthinkable loss.

The doctors don't yet have an explanation for why this baby died. When you see him, it makes sense why Deborah warned you, but he's really not that bad. His head looks like a kneecap with colorless eyes, but his body is mostly intact. You're able to get more than just his feet. You come away with a few good shots of his torso, thumb, jawline.

After the shoot, Deborah approaches you and Ellen in the hallway. "How active are you in the birthing community?" she asks.

"This is the extent of it," says Ellen.

"Don't you think it would be good to see the other side of things?" she says. "You could help launch some families that have had—how do I say it—better fortune."

It's a good idea, but you're not sure how to say so. You look into an empty suite, toward wallpapered walls of soft leaves and berries.

"These experiences have a way of becoming a part of you," she cautions. Then she hands you her business card, smiling like she just invited you to church.

At the time, what you say to Deborah is that school is about to start—you'll be very busy. But on the first day of class, you wash your face in the sink, listen to professors read their syllabi, then eat lunch in the basement cafeteria where the international students hang out. Sure, getting kicked out of BOK means you have no friends, but you're also free from Greek life and its carnival routines. No mandatory kayaking trips. No parties where you're handed a liter of spiced rum and a bendy straw. No "community service" party buses taking everyone to the animal shelter so you can pet kittens for two hours, then attack each other with lint rollers in the parking lot. When you accept being at the bottom of the social hierarchy, college actually requires very little of your time and bears even less on your identity.

So you call Deborah. You meet her at the store she owns, a natural parenting boutique on MLK that shares a parking lot with Bruno's Used Tires and the only Thai restaurant in town. First, she loans you some books. You read about vitamin K injections, neuraxial analgesia, malpositioned babies. Then about the C-section boom, female hysteria, sexual politics of fertility. In one book, you flip through sketches of genderless cartoons holding pregnant women, stretching their limbs, slow dancing, giving them perineal massages. It tells you to accept your body for the hormonal soup that it is. Of course, all of this is a big time commitment, but Deborah doesn't doubt you, doesn't talk down to you like a lovable naïf. When you come back, she is sitting on the floor, inexplicably wearing tight jeans and a giant cardigan in boiling September heat. She looks like a cat that's been resting in a panel of sunlight, and beneath her blithe demeanor, there's a sort of heroic poise. You want to get close enough to be calibrated, like a tuning fork.

Later on, you're reading a book that addresses non-biological motherhood, and it starts listing all the ways that you (a presumed adoptive/foster/stepmother) will not be granted the rights afforded to women who procreate. Your child will view you as an interloper, it says. She will be wrestling with a maternal ghost. She will keep a critical distance from you. She will fetishize the biological—and so on. To manage this, the book suggests that you view your womb as a liminal space, functioning as a portal between real and symbolic offspring. "Consider that you were born alongside your child the moment you first met," it says.

Invariably, these ideas smear themselves onto your foster parents—whom you refer to as Abby and Henry, not Mom or Dad. It exposes how you still view them as diffident schoolteachers who don't love you in the "real" way. How their home was just a vessel for your suffering—that house on Fauntleroy, with its dead rose bushes, monogrammed towels, their old poodle named Cato. How caring for a grieving child must have been exacting and unrewarding work. In fact, you never even asked them why they didn't have children before you—or if they did, what happened. You feel so selfish. You put the book away, but at night you dream of approaching Abby in the kitchenette, where she turns to you ceremoniously. "I have his ashes in a jar in my hope chest," she says. And when you try to respond, the night sky approaches the window like a falling anvil.

That weekend, you drive home, and as you pass all the sordid yards with cars leaking fluid, the boulder on which the mayor annually paints JESUS SAVES, you prepare a speech. In this speech, you admit to your parents you treated them poorly, that you avoided facing what seemed outside your understanding. But when you get there, Henry is raking wet leaves in the yard, and he waves like you're in a pageant. He takes you into your dustless room where your sheets are freshly ironed. Then into the kitchen, where Cato licks your palms, and Abby asks you to chop something for dinner. It's harder than you thought to escape your baked-in teenage role. By the time you sit down for dinner, you decide against the speech entirely. After all, you are just now learning the trap that loss has put you in, and the speech would be a lie—it would be announcing that you have already escaped, when clearly, you haven't.

So you resolve to spend more time with your parents. You keep meeting with Deborah. You try to trust your own decisions. Then one day, you are walking back to your dorm from class, passing the library, which is no longer shuttered with white sheets, and you find a small group of people have gathered by the fountain. They are chanting I BELIEVE THAT WE WILL WIN, holding signs that say 1000% DEATH PENALTY and ENCARSERATION ISN'T ENOUGH. The governor recently told prosecutors to seek the death penalty for Eli, which means his picture is everywhere again—the vacant, frizzy-haired one, where he's leering toward the camera in a padded vest. You remember he lost his mother at age eleven (the same time you lost yours), and that this fact is often cited as a reason for his depravity. You wonder if he, too, continually struggled to find words for this loss. If he avoided thinking of himself as a short-handed child or a victim. You wonder if he let these things live completely unsaid, so by the time he arrived at OU, the luxury of college felt both sinister and false. You sit on a bench so long the protestors disperse. Dusk folds over campus like a giant wave. You think maybe you should be ashamed, comparing yourself to a mass murderer. But instead, you see it as a way to move forward. You are learning that to admit your darkest self will bring you into a world you had only partially entered.

Then in October, you meet a guy named Scott Gilson. At first, you simply know him as the one senior in your geology class, the thin guy with a wobbly leg, shop glasses, an abandoned attempt at a curly mohawk.

But then the *Ozarka Times* puts his face on the cover of the Sunday newspaper. SHOOTING SURVIVOR HEALS THROUGH ART, it declares. And then you realize—he was the guy who was shot through the back, trampled, given a news conference when updated from critical to stable, who has a piece of bullet permanently embedded in his rib. The article announces his senior art show, which is happening at a campus gallery, though it doesn't say much about his art. It mostly describes the grisly aftermath of the shooting. The months he spent convalescing at home. The abdominal binder that held his organs in place, the incessant calls from *Good Morning America*. It just says he worked his way back from therapeutic coloring books to sculpture. In the sidebar, they publish a photo of him standing in his yard before an outbuilding, next to a steel cage shaped like a bull. He looks ruddy and charming.

The show happens on a gray afternoon filled with hatches of flies, revving leaf blowers, the daylight already threatened by what will be a prompt, dark winter. You show up with your camera. You want to appear artistic and deliberate—not some stranger with a perverse attraction to Scott's public persona of survivorhood (though, to be honest, that's partly why you're here).

Inside the gallery, there are giant bowls of sugary cereal and jugs of milk on ice, which means everyone is slurping Lucky Charms and Froot Loops while staring at the sculptures. In the center of the room, there's a plaster cast of a human body strung up on rope, holding reins attached to two baying wolves made entirely of razor wire. There's a dead-eyed stag made out of black rope, and a steel bull, its insides now filled with teddy bears wearing Christmas sweaters. Everything is festooned with artificial flowers. They are titled *Vox Nihili, Hoc Est Corpus, In Absentia.*

When you see Scott, he's wearing an ugly brown suit, answering questions about his pieces, gesturing to them broadly like a deranged car salesman. You point your camera at axe heads, rotten lace, Styrofoam, deer remains. You think about trauma taking a physical shape, shadows growing out of sculptures like ectoplasmic specters.

Eventually, Scott goes over to the cereal bar, mixes all of them into the same bowl, then stands in the corner, eating with his head down. You approach him and introduce yourself, but you don't know what to say.

"What's your major?" he asks.

"Poultry Science, but I might change it to Nursing."

"So you want to be a nurse."

"Not really."

He looks around the room, takes a step like he's about to wander off.

"These sculptures remind me of memorials," you say eventually. "All the flowers and random material."

Scott shakes his head. "People keep telling me that. But the thing is—I made most everything before the shooting. I bought two hundred fake flowers at Hobby Lobby last November. It's starting to freak me out."

You want to say you meant any memorial. Marking highway car crashes, dirt road cemeteries, woven into fences lined with tornado rubble. But then again, you can't blame him for being defensive, for not wanting this event to become some kumbaya-type moment. You know all too well that when a community tries this hard to "come together," it ends up isolating those closest to the tragedy, only uniting those on the outside who—for some god forsaken reason—are trying to become part of the club.

"So, what's it about then?"

"I don't know," Scott says, taking a bite of his cereal. "Animal mythologies. Diametrically opposed mediums. Shit like that." He reaches into his pocket and pulls out a pink gemstone. "Here," he says. "For you."

You turn the gemstone over in your hand. It's definitely plastic, with worn-out adhesive on the back—the type of thing that might have come off a child's backpack.

"Thanks," you say.

Recently, you've been drawn to guys like Scott because you're rebelling against the type of man you've been taught to desire: that Mr. Potato Head of wealth, arrogance, and style you idolized when you came to college. That's why you noticed him in class. But now, his art and his history have triangulated him into a very serious crush. You sit next to him in class. You show him the pictures you took of his art show, and when he says the color is a little off, you say, "A photograph is an interpretation, asshole." When you walk out together, he lifts up his shirt and shows you the pink seam running across his torso. He tells you about voicemails from sympathetic strangers, the condolence letter he received from the president. You talk about pregnancy, then sit beside each other as your professor lectures on opposing geological theories. She asks, "Were the Earth's prominent features formed by violent geologic shifts, or slowly over time?" The class votes, and she shakes her head. "Do you know why it's so hard for the scientific community to convince people of the gradual shifts?" she says. "Because nothing fossilizes unless you bury it rapidly. The Earth is designed to remember one thing and forget the other."

Later on, you are walking up the big hill toward campus when Scott pulls ahead of you in his car, a maroon minivan with a garbage bag for a rear window. He offers you a ride to class, and when you get in the passenger seat, you find one of those teddy bears from his art show. He tells you to keep it, says there are five thousand more of them in a warehouse on the east side of town. And when you express disbelief, he takes a turn in the opposite direction of campus, then gets on the bypass. He drives by trailer repair shops, vacant lots, a billboard that says JESUS IS PLAN A, THERE IS NO PLAN B. He parks at a distribution warehouse next to a tractor supply company.

Inside, you meet a guy named Roger, the county's tax assessor who was hired to sort through all the donations that poured in after the shooting. He has a black goatee and bleary eyes. He says he's happy to see anyone that isn't FedEx. He shows you across the glossy cement, past thousands of paper cranes, patchwork quilts, bicycles, and Christmas ornaments. He says there's mail from fifty states and eighty countries. There are banners signed by schoolchildren in Shanghai. A NASCAR racing hood. Hand-crocheted army fatigues. There are boxes of Cheerios, Yankee candles, angel wings, baseballs, unbuilt IKEA furniture. There's a desk and a photocopy machine, which belongs to an anthropology professor who has been cataloging all the handwritten letters. Then, in a room with multi-hued pallets wrapped in plastic, you find the tier of teddy bears, all wearing the same red Christmas sweaters emblazoned with the star of Bethlehem.

"What's going to happen to all of this?" you ask.

"I wish I knew," says Roger. "We're having a hell of a time getting rid of it." He walks over to a bin and pulls out a paper snowflake, then puts it back. "There's been talk of hauling it to an incinerator. I mean, I think we could do it in a nice way, like a ceremony. But at this point, this stuff is just a reminder. Everyone wants to move on."

You look over at Scott, but his back is turned, arms crossed.

After this, you don't go home, and you don't go back to campus. Scott drives you to his house at the edge of town where the sidewalks disappear, down a dirt road that leads through a shipwrecked yard, the burned shell of a Mercedes, toward a cottage with several generations of satellite dishes bolted to the roof. This moment marks what you will later regard as the beginning of your relationship. Not because you confessed your love to each other, or because you kissed or had sex, but because you are beginning to realize just how numb and insulated Scott really is, and he has chosen you to witness this.

He shows you around the house. You meet Sarah, his bug-eyed pit bull. You see the garage sale recliner he used as an ad hoc hospital bed. His mom comes over from the property down the street, fixes ice tea, warns Scott there will be several loud bangs from her breaking apart ice cubes in the kitchen. Later, when you begin staying the night, Scott grabs a baseball bat, uses it as a cane while he secures the perimeter of the house. Everything is so dark. The house is filled with dim lamps. Out back there's a murky pond surrounded by switch willows, where even the moon seems to be missing from the sky. Out here, beyond the wall of forest, there's just one fractal pattern of vague stars.

Then in November, almost exactly a month before the anniversary of the shooting, there's another one at a community college in New Mexico. When you first hear the news, you go over to Scott's house and find him eating ice cream on the couch, watching an old surveillance video he got from a friend that works at a gas station. The footage shows him walking into the store, buying a Red Bull, then drinking it as he fills up his van.

"I can't move like that anymore," he says. He stands up and mimes purchasing the drink and pushing open a door. As he walks across the living room, there is a barely perceptible click in his hip, like it's on a mechanical hinge.

"Looks the same to me," you say.

"Really?" he says. He does his routine all over again, but this time there's one big click that interrupts the rhythm of his steps. "Fuck!" he screams. He starts punching the side of his leg.

By the time you reach him, his hands are covering his face, and he collapses onto the couch. For a long time, you don't speak. You rub his back and look out the window, where clouds stumble drowsy over the arched mountains.

Eventually, Scott slackens. "I turned on the TV and some news panel was explaining how to survive an active shooter scenario," he says. "One of them suggested people shield themselves with dead bodies."

That night, the two of you don't even try to sleep. Scott goes out into the living room, knocks over a bookshelf, then cuts it in half with a circular saw. He flips over the couch, taking pliers to each staple in the fabric, twists out every screw, and with the remaining material he makes a low-lying gazebo fort, with floor-to-ceiling cushions. You crawl in there together and have one of those conversations where nothing is sacred anymore. You talk to each other about how to cope when your body feels vandalized. When you're afraid of what your mind remembers. When every day you are snatching your life from the thing that tried to destroy it. Scott describes reciting his birthday while medics wheeled him into the hospital, having dreams of being stepped on, exploding tiles, the whiteness of brain matter. You start talking about barkless trees, unstable skies, the gunshots of policemen euthanizing injured horses, but then you stop yourself. You're starting to learn to help others not by exchanging your trauma, but by offering them the patience and understanding you once needed, but didn't get.

When morning comes, Scott starts putting the living room back together, and in the end it looks almost exactly as it did, minus the new seams and loosened fabric. At this moment, a particular thought emerges that you will keep with you for the rest of your life:

the idea that two bodies can move through different lives in the same way. That the trauma you go through can, if anything, prepare you to understand someone else. You keep this thought to yourself not because you are ashamed or because you don't think it's important, but because you don't want to give anyone the opportunity to negotiate you out of believing it.

You're able to maintain your sanity because, in addition to Scott, you also have Ellen, Deborah, and your parents. You change your major, decorate your apartment. You go home, drink margaritas with Abby and Henry. You stand above a woman crying in a tub, learning how to count contractions, and you keep stepping into the strange portal that pregnancy opens up for you. In other words, you have your own life. You are not carving out space to exist within other people. You're not looking at the world through a prearranged peephole. You do not view Scott's pain as your own, and you do not try to fix it, because you can't.

And you are going to need all of these things, because in a few months, Eli's criminal trial will begin. Scott will use the rest of his victim restitution money (most of which paid his medical bills) to get the nicest hotel room he can find, where he will stay for almost three weeks, going through every painstaking detail of the shooting. He will watch Eli swivel absently in an office chair, wearing a partially unbuttoned dress shirt that's just a little too dashing for a murder trial. He will listen to a geneticist explain individual-level abnormalities in violent criminals, to attorneys surmising that Eli did something cruel because he didn't know what cruelty looked like. Scott will latch onto these explanations, hoping they will clarify why the shooting happened. You, on the other hand, already know that a different, simpler, and more relatable explanation has been out there this whole time, living like a creak in an old house everyone has learned to ignore.

FELICIANA

ELI

You're able to drive far into night. The bridges of I-49 carry you over valleys then back up into mountains, past unclassifiable churches, confused deer on the roadside, and through yellow pines that hang over the road like a vaulted ceiling. But the farther you get, the more you feel disappointed, passing through towns that the news of the shooting has not yet reached. You drive in packs of somnambulant cars, bathed in acrid sweat and unnatural silence. You turn on the radio and a voice explains how scientists are immunizing frogs against a deadly fungus. You drift onto rumble strips, staring too long into your rearview, hoping the lights of patrol cars will interrupt the dark so you can surrender. After all, you wouldn't want to get away even if you could. You wouldn't want to leap back over the walls of power and meaning that you burst through—the ones you'd been standing outside of for so long.

You drive so far south the highway terminates, and you take an interchange that spits you out onto a winding road into Oklahoma. There's no such thing as a wrong turn for you at this point, but that's how it feels. You're alone, driving through speed zones in slim daylight, past creeks that end in piles of trash, fences decorated with artillery shells, sporadic mailboxes half devoured by foliage. Eventually, you enter a town called Moyer Springs, which prides itself on being the hometown of John Johnson, a famous NASCAR driver. On the main strip, you pass the John Johnson museum, which is actually just a glass structure attached to a used car dealership that contains an old stock car. It's here that police cars finally converge behind you, dashcams watching as you pull lazily onto the gravel shoulder, then come to a stop.

A triangle of officers approaches you, guns drawn, walking through roadside grass exploding with crickets.

"Hands up," yells the foremost officer, but your hands are already raised. He approaches your door while the others stay back. When you meet, he lowers his gun and holsters it, which makes you suddenly aware of your appearance—a sleep-deprived young man in an American Eagle T-shirt, hair curling out at his ears, a hint of a beard. You can almost see your reflection in his root-beer-colored sunglasses, but ropes of headlights and sirens flash across them in every direction.

This is how they arrest you, in a way that is cold, recited, and gentle. The cops help you out of the car, take your driver's license out of your pocket, cuff you, then pat you down again. They put you in the back of a squad car that smells of air freshener, fast food, and hot vinyl. A barely audible Allman Brothers song plays on the radio. You sit there for a long time as they search your BMW, talk on the radio, and give each other congratulatory fist bumps. At one point, an officer crawls out of the backseat holding a chicken feather, and for a moment you can hear a flapping sound in the other room as Gordon falls onto a pile of clothes, then rolls onto his side, trying to stand back up. For the first time, it occurs to you that Gordon might have survived. You left without checking his pulse, assuming a close-range shot to the chest would be fatal. But would it? You consider this for a second, then decide to avoid reaching farther back into that moment. If you're going to feel sad or scared, you must do so in a secret place that even you cannot enter. If anything, you should thank Gordon, because before that moment you were still one of those people who had never done anything—right or wrong—that mattered very much.

They take you to a station in Oklahoma where you briefly appear before a judge, then you get sent back over the border in an unmarked minivan surrounded by a convoy of patrol cars that drive through flat pastureland and dead industrial towns. A billboard declares SE-CEDE in bold letters. Once in Ozarka, they put you in a tiny room that's decorated like the lobby of an investment company—blue carpet, a green lamp on a faux-oak side table. Two detectives tie what look like microwaveable popcorn bags over each of your hands to preserve gunshot residue, then they leave you alone for hours. They come back with a Happy Meal and a tiny soda. They take the bags off your hands and let you eat in silence, and when you're done, you reach into the box and find a small cat figurine with kindhearted eyes and a pink bow, one hand frozen in a wave.

"Sorry," says one of the detectives. "We're going to need that."

You slide it across the table. He regards it with a smile, then puts it in his shirt pocket. "You good to talk?"

You're prepared to explain how no one cared or listened, so you chose to terrorize the world with what it created, but the detectives only ask questions that invite tepid little responses. How do you spell your name? What type of car were you driving? How many doors does it have? Are you allergic to anything? Why drive to Oklahoma? Aren't the ponderosa pines beautiful this time of year? They leave and come back. Why did you park in the fire lane? Have you spent much time in the library? What books have you been reading? When you brought the rifle to your shoulder, did you target specific people? Do you remember the color of the sky? You mean a strong red, like crimson, or a lighter one, such as pink?

When they're done asking questions, two guards wearing flak jackets escort you down the hall, shine a flashlight in your eyes while you strip, then put you in a shower where water comes up to your ankles. When you're done, they give you a baggy jail jumpsuit that makes you look like a beige penguin, then walk you out to a three-tiered mezzanine where voices clang off metal and concrete. Your cell is a desk, a bed with a wool blanket, and a sink/toilet combination. Once inside, you read the disciplinary codebook out of boredom, overhear a woman yelling at prison guards, saying handcuffs gave her AIDS. When you look out your window, all you can see is a coterie of officers, and another prisoner in his cell who appears to be knitting. You watch him until he looks back at you and stands up to mime holding a baseball bat. You think it might be part of a game until he swings downward, as if on top of someone's head. He looks at you again and pretends to hold someone's throat while punching through their stomach. He throws the body to the ground, straddles it on his knees, and keeps punching.

It's not long before you can see the glacier of time that has amassed before you. You have no concept of how much time has elapsed, or how much will. You try to fight against your boredom. You examine the folds of your clothes, roll up your sleeves, balance a paper cup on your head, chew on a wad of it like bubblegum. You focus so hard on the blotches in the wall that when a tray holding apple slices and a sandwich appears through a slot on the door, you don't grab it right away, and it disappears. You hide from the bleaching lights under your blanket and try to think about how you've successfully inverted the order of the world, but your mind is traveling toward the edges of your pride, where guilt resides. It puts you in a boat with your father, feet wet, wearing his jacket that smells like sweat and drywall. It wakes you up in the morning to the sound of Gordon crushing beer cans in the backyard. It wonders what thought was interrupted as he turned to you, as if having reached the edge of a dream. But you push aside each memory until you are a slab, a head of cabbage in a garden, just a territory of light or sound.

You wake up to the sound of officers unlocking your cell door. They take you down a long hallway and shove you into another room, alone, still shackled with handcuffs, a belly chain, and leg irons. The room is empty, with cement walls enlarged by sunlight that make you feel you've entered a different climate, like you just walked into a desert. At one end of the room is a glass partition, and beyond it sit a dozen scattered plastic chairs. You shuffle closer and see a young man in the back, pacing the wall and holding a binder of paperwork. He wears a baggy sportcoat, his hair spiked and prematurely graying. When he sees you, he grabs a chair and carries it toward the glass.

"Who are you?"

He sits down, leans into an opening in the glass. "Hello, Eli," he says. "I'll be representing you." He looks at his watch. "Better take a seat—we only have a couple minutes."

He says his name is Ashley Finn, asks if you were read your Miranda rights, and that's when the room starts to pivot. A low-frequency wind picks up and howls against your back. But Ashley keeps talking. He says something about a criminal extradition act. An arraignment. Do you know your father's cell phone number? How long did you speak to detectives? Then something about charging papers. Twelve counts murder in the first degree. Sixty-seven criminal. Flips through all the pages. Make sure you understand these when we go in there, he says. Respond, "Your honor." Don't look around too much. Keep your eyes downcast. Something about no bond being set. No grand jury. Hey, are you doing okay?

You realize you've begun rocking rhythmically in your chair. You stop.

He says one more thing—something about soliciting the help of another attorney. Susan King. New York. *Pro hac vice,* so it will be a few days before you meet. Lots of experience with the death penalty. Pro bono. Never lost a case. Not as far as he knows. Hey, guards are coming. (Keys clang on the other side of the door). He'll be taking care of everything from now on. Don't talk to anyone. Are you ready?

Ashley stands up and the guards come in. You don't move, just sit there staring at him, and for a moment you slip into the rapids of his eyes. You could ask him if Gordon is dead, but at this point, you'd rather not know. Gordon was supposed to be sacrificed, and therefore spared. If he's alive, there's simply nowhere in the world he'd belong.

"It will be okay," says Ashley. "You should stand up, though. It's a *go-or-be-taken* type of place."

The courtroom is smaller than you expected, and when you enter, you look out into the public gallery at the families, assembled media, and sketch artists lining the wooden benches. Several women wear pink ribbons in memoriam. Just before you turn your back, you find your father's emaciated face.

A deputy stands so close you can feel his breath as the judge reads counts against you. Slowly, you slip into a vortex of light above him, which grows until the ceiling unglues itself and slips into the sky.

"Yes, your honor."

It isn't until you're back in your cell that you realize you're holding Ashley's business card. You don't know when it was given to you. A voice starts wailing through the sink again, and for the first time you realize what's happening. You have completed the process of drawing away from experience, from other people, and toward yourself—toward death. This thought will bracket every emotion, even guilt, for the rest of your life.

A few days later, a guard opens your cell and, instead of taking you to the rec yard—which is just a tiny basketball court with a sign that says 67 LAPS=1 MILE—he takes you to the visitation room. It's an open cafeteria-like space with numbers hanging above tables. Your father is sitting at number twelve, hands folded, hair dented by the buffalo-hide cowboy hat he tried to wear into the facility. A smog-colored window blunts the sunlight behind him.

Already, you're anticipating the lecture he is about to give. He will ask why you couldn't find nothing else to do with your life, then he will recall some specific moment in the past, like when he was fixing the expansion valve on the truck and spilled Freon on his face. Do you remember driving me to the hospital? he will say. How you slung my arm around your shoulder? Where is that person? What happened to him? He will try to take you to someplace in the past, like that garage lit up by Christmas lights in the rafters, the explosive voices of college football on the radio, in order to castigate you with the present.

But he doesn't say any of this. When you sit down, he makes his hand into a fist and blocks half of his face, which seems to have lost all its familiar edges.

"I always felt like I loved you in a way that meant I constantly feared your destruction," he says. "Maybe you're just that type of kid. Maybe all parents feel this way. But now, it's like I didn't fear carefully enough. I didn't know I had to imagine such a wide latitude of pain."

Beside you, a small child is whipping a chair with a beaded necklace while her parents talk, seemingly bored by her Sunday obligation.

"Anyway," your father says, "this Susan King we got to defend you is a big deal." He starts listing off the books she's written and the people she's defended—which, if you were listening, you'd realize includes a bomber of abortion clinics, a white supremacist who shot up a synagogue, and a canal worker who drowned human cargo. But you're not listening, because now you're worried your father is only shocked by how you chose to express your misery, not that you were miserable in the first place. It's like he already gave up and surrendered to a moment like this one a long time ago.

"She's going to be looking for all the mitigating factors," your father says.

"Mitigating factors," you repeat.

"The insanity defense is just trying to rehumanize you, in any way we can. Because out there, you're already a monster. The things people are saying about you—" He trails off.

You both look at the clock in the back of the room. A guard comes by and tells your father not to cross his legs.

"Look me in the eyes, Eli."

You look.

"I'm heartbroken," he says. "That this happened. That something was missing, or taken from you."

"Nothing was taken from me," you say.

He pauses, like some imaginary thing is growing before him until it's real, and it's sealing you inside. Then he shakes it off.

"You have what you need in here?"

"It's hard to feel anything."

"Right. Well, I heard you can buy books and snacks from the commissary if I put some money in your account."

Guards are shouting orders now, unlocking doors.

Before your father leaves, you stand up. "Dad," you say, and you almost tell him you are sorry, but you know that word is a trap. To acknowledge what you did had no justification would be to risk total self-annihilation. So instead you say "Thanks," though you're not sure what it means, or how it might be interpreted.

Each day, you wake up with the lights already on, and the room expands around you. You do pushups, masturbate, stare at the wall until you start seeing things. A wormhole of concentric circles. Boxy reptiles marching around the periphery. You watch the guards like television. The blond-haired guy everyone calls "Superman." The woman with fake eyelashes. A court-appointed psychologist comes by, gives you a full-scale IQ test. He has a shaved head, designer tortoiseshell glasses, begins every sentence by saying "I don't mean to put words in your mouth, but…" Eventually, you get access to the library, and you half-read all the Dickens novels and GED Test Prep booklets until you get a copy of *The Diary of a Young Girl*. You read it in one sitting, wait until time flattens out, and then read it again. You imagine that Anne Frank is there, in your cell. "I keep trying to find a way to become myself," she says, "but there are so many people preventing me." She stares through the slit in your window at the guards like they are dirty children on the streets of Prinsengracht.

That night, the guards call you for a shower, which you're always escorted to alone since you're still in protective custody. While soaping your hair, you close your eyes, imagining that you're bathing in Anne Frank's front office, scrubbing yourself at night so the fascists don't hear you. That's when the room turns horizontal. For some reason, your face is against the wall, and when you turn around, another prisoner is there. His fist smashes your throat, permanently damaging your larynx, then as you collapse into the shallow water, his punches swing into the empty air where your face used to be. He grabs onto the showerhead for stability, then starts kicking your curled-up body.

"Stop fighting!" yells a guard.

The guy's heel comes down on your shoulder, then your ribs. "Fuck you," he says. "Fuck you fuck you fuck you." You breathe in water until you're falling through the tile, into a wave of sharp edges.

When the story breaks, the man who assaulted you becomes an overnight Internet sensation. People find out he's been in jail eighteen months for strong-armed robbery, so they start a campaign called FREE GARY MURDOCK that describes him as a national hero, gathers $50,000 in bail money. The sheriff comes by after you're discharged from the medical unit. He apologizes, says one of the guards who was supposed to be watching you was on lunch break, while the other was handing toilet paper to another inmate. When you ask how Murdock got out of his cell in the first place, the sheriff says if you want to press charges, you should speak to your attorney.

The next day, you're escorted through a subterranean hallway in the jail that you've never seen before, then deposited in a pale blue room that looks like it functions as a chapel. Inside, Susan is standing next to an empty table wearing a dour pantsuit, her hair cut in a professional sullen bob.

"Are you okay?" She touches her neck as if imagining your bruises are her own. When she says this, you feel a sort of long-lost intimacy. You realize how quiet it is, away from the din of voices on the cellblock. You notice how there's no paperwork, no notepads or voice recorders on the table. And when you tell her about your swollen neck and possible laryngeal fracture, she seems genuinely concerned, leaning toward you to listen, her cuffed sleeves revealing the ultraviolet stamp on her wrist that security gives to each visitor.

This is the moment when you realize Susan might be your last personal connection. It's why you agree not to press charges, hoping if the public already feels they've scored a victory, maybe they'll be less likely to sentence you to death. It's why you tell her about drawing a bath so you could scream underwater after your mother died. How Gordon stood on the couch and ranted about the US government importing thirty thousand guillotines in preparation for martial law. How you lost all your money. It's why you hold your gut, say you're condemned to be a slim version of yourself. You can feel it—and all of the future—inside of you. It's why you trust her to sit through the silences you create, looking around the room like some calm but erudite animal, listening for something no one else can hear.

But this connection only lasts so long. After several visits, Susan goes back to New York and does her work there until the trial. You feel abandoned. You call her and she doesn't answer. Instead of coming back, she hires a social worker to help your father create a psychosocial history of your life. They interview everyone you've ever known. They fill banker's boxes with mitigating evidence—old report cards, your mother's food stamp paperwork, news articles of her car wreck, your father's discharge papers from the army, short stories, journal entries. They say they're trying to work the following angles: you were a wayward child, you were saddled with disenfranchised grief, you have substance abuse issues, you are floridly psychotic/schizoaffective/narcissistic, and your ability to cope was like a gas tank that eventually ran dry.

They hire a guy named Dr. Schlessinger who visits you, radiating musk, and asks questions like: Do you think dependency is dysfunctional? Do you feel devalued as a human? When your mom was alive, how did your parents resolve conflict? Eventually, you start to resent them all for thinking the narrative of your life is just out there for the taking. They don't actually want to help you or know you. They just want to preserve their own ideas of compassion and meaning. They want to hold onto the vast practical joke of their lives so they don't have to feel the pain and confusion its absence would reveal. And they don't care if you die. They just want you to believe your crime was the result of a tortured psyche. There's nothing cruel about death—only misunderstanding, and that is exactly how they are planning to empty you.

A year goes by, and as you wait for the trial, time slips completely off its flimsy edifice, taking with it all the intervals that create a life. Jail traps you into one long, weak season. A lost spacecraft. A boat on a planet of water.

During this time, you manage your anxiety about the trial by cataloging all your memories. You mentally organize all the books you've read, the best meals you ate, the camping trips you took. The category you spend the longest time accessing is girls you've liked. The one you carpooled with in middle school. The one you took into the horse stalls at the fairgrounds. You exhaust every acquaintance, then drift into scenes of half-remembered girls. The cashier at Savers Club. The one who dressed up as Emily Dickinson in English 120.

In one of these memories, you're walking up Arkansas Avenue toward class, passing a white sorority house stranded in a giant green lawn. It's ten in the morning, but a red carpet spills from its French doors. Several girls wearing matching white mini dresses stand alongside the carpet. As they clap their hands to a song, you wait at a crosswalk, trying to pick out your favorite, when a shorter, dark-complexioned girl appears in the doorframe. Her hair is in a fishtail braid, and there's something different about her face, though you're too far away to decide what. As she joins the row with choreographed flair, you wonder what it must feel like to be so perfect, and accepted, and innocent. Later, returning to this memory several times, you imagine where this girl is now. You figure she's about to graduate, take some parent-funded vacation to Paris, get engaged, open a clothing boutique downtown. You feel so cheated, that someone could be given such a life, while you're here.

Eventually, Susan decides against another continuance, sends out all her subpoenas, and coaches you about trial etiquette. You pack your belongings in an industrial-sized garbage bag, get escorted off the cellblock and into a garage full of patrol cars. When you leave, you expect to see some kind of daylight, especially since you just ate breakfast. But the door opens to the middle of the night. No sunlight climbing hills. No clouds. No heat. Just faint moonshadows. Tree branches twining in the dark.

You spend what feels like a day in a holding cell in the bowels of the courthouse, and then the trial begins. When you enter, the courtroom is not the big adversarial space you imagined. No intricate wainscoting, balustraded railings, or high-canopied ceilings. No judge dictating from a bench of imposing proportions. It's just a small rectangular box lined with plastic office chairs and a few rows of interlocking benches for audience seating. The judge, a small blond woman who speaks with some accent or lisp you can't identify, sits before a wood panel, flanked by two large flatscreen monitors.

Clerks and attorneys are hunched over their laptops surrounded by paper coffee cups. It doesn't make you feel elevated or symbolic—it makes you feel like you're about to take a standardized test in a garish townhome.

As the judge introduces the case and goes over courtroom protocol, you start to worry about your appearance. You've gained some weight in the last year, so the dress shirt your father brought fits tight around your waist. You were told not to smile or frown, but also not to look flat or unemotional. You look over at the five sharply dressed prosecutors, and beyond them the jurors' box, the forewoman in a purple suit and white scarf. She's already crossing her arms at you. You glance at the crowd, which is a collage of unrecognizable faces. You pour yourself some water, trying to look nonchalant, but you can't shake the feeling Gordon is here somewhere. You imagine him in the back corner, partially reclined in a platform wheelchair. You swear you can feel the heat of his stare on the back of your neck.

Eventually, one of the prosecutors stands for his opening statement. He faces the jurors, presses a remote, and a high-definition photograph of Reid Library appears on the screen. A carpet of dead leaves leads up to its grey stone façade. Yellow windows erupt with light.

"On a cold December evening," he says, "not far from where we sit today, over three hundred kids were packed in this library. All that love and hope, just beyond those doors." He pauses, lets silence fill the room, and then presses the button again, at which point the screen goes black. The deep static of a student calling 911 plays, with gunshots and screaming in the background, and then the phone cuts off.

He tells the jury that you are legally sane. You killed people to increase your self-worth. He reads from your ninth-grade notebook, picking a line where you claim there are no absolute moral standards. While he talks, names of victims scroll across the screen. He says you have a longstanding hatred of mankind. He references something you said in probably the twenty-second hour of your interview with

Dr. Schlessinger, when you started rambling about numbers, saying each person you killed was a point, while each wounded was "just collateral damage." He explains how you stole from Gordon, how you stole from Ramon, how you were a misanthrope and a drug dealer, how you refused antipsychotic drugs after your arrest. He says you are smart. You planned. Your entire life was a subterfuge. He says: we must hold you accountable, then he clicks again and a portrait of Gordon appears. He's leaning against a vending machine in a hall you've never seen before.

"Eli murdered his best friend," he says. "It was his first act."

This is one of many opportunities you've had to believe that Gordon is dead. But you've been shaping the story of his survival for so long that no matter what, it still *feels* like what really happened. Your mind mutates "murdered his best friend" into "*tried to murder* his best friend," until the original remark gets stamped with the insignia of a dream.

When the prosecutor steps down, it's Susan's turn. She stands behind a lectern that faces the jury box, describing your mother's death, saying fear was taken away from you when you were young. She says you were so alone your thoughts hardened into delusions. You heard a voice. You were robbed of your own reality. You created loss to be reunified with your mother. She reads the reports from your first days in jail. Inmate seen licking walls. Lying naked on the floor, eating a paper cup. Inmate seen performing a "trust fall" alone, arms outstretched on edge of his bed. Inmate seen hiding under blanket. Hiding under sheet. Hiding under fitted sheet. Hiding under mattress. She says that when you were losing the struggle with psychosis, you turned to drugs to self-medicate. You sent your father an email saying you had fun hiking to Hawksbill Crag with your girlfriend, when in fact you had no girlfriend. These, she says, are actions that have fluidity within your disease. Shyness. Awkwardness. Decline in function. The rest of the time, you were just functional enough to employ sane

behaviors in service of your delusions. So by the time you reached the
library, you weren't seeking a battle. You had already lost one.

Day one of the trial ends, and as a black light gets thrown onto
your entire life, you feel like everyone has missed the point entirely.
The whole idea behind the shooting was that you had never done
anything wrong. You weren't evil or psychotic. You were overlooked,
disenfranchised, promised one thing and given another. The only
thing that should be discussed is how strong your impulse became to
release this pain back out into the world.

But the trial moves on. For the next two weeks, the prosecu-
tion calls witnesses. First, it's the survivors. They talk about jumping over bodies, sitting on curbs, wrapping shredded jeans around
their legs, running past fire trucks, their flip-flops slipping in blood.
They are shown photographs of friends in the ICU, describe the
bodies and furniture that broke their falls. Shattered kidneys. Follow-up surgeries. Scar tissue sealing in shrapnel. The prosecutor
hands them tissues. He pulls back a student's hair so the jurors can
see her disfigured neck. He asks: Does this photo accurately rep-
resent how your friend looked just before brain surgery? At what
point did you realize you were paralyzed from the waist down? Is
that your dead daughter's green scarf you are wearing? He asks Eddie: Who is that in the picture, up there, beside you in her hiking
gear? He asks Scott: Do you even celebrate Christmas anymore?
He asks Gordon's mother: Do you feel like you've lost what you
were put on this earth to do—raise your child? A medical examiner
describes the impact of a bullet when it enters a body. A surgeon
explains how a hospital went code black, threw away thirty pizzas
someone delivered because they were afraid they'd been poisoned.
Police officers describe the library floor coated in casings. The fluorescent fire alarm flashing all night. The patrol cars driving over
curbs and through campus gardens. A deputy explains how, once
the story broke, there was a moment in the library when the first

cell phone started ringing, then another, then eventually the whole empty building was buzzing with parents and friends calling these kids who weren't going to answer.

At some point near the end of all this, I get called to the stand. The prosecutor asks me closed-ended questions about your writing abilities, trying to make you appear smart and deliberate. Would you say Eli's ability to express himself on the page was above average? Did he seem passionate about his work? On the assignments he completed, he received excellent grades, did he not?

But after he's done, Susan stands up, and for the first time, she cross-examines a witness. She asks me about that time you came to my office.

"Dr. Bressinger," she says, "did Eli seem like the kind of student who could arrive at a firm evaluation of what he has done?"

The answer, of course, is no. But that's not exactly what I say. Because at this point in my life, I hate you. I am worried about Eddie. I think that extending any empathy or understanding toward you would be the surest way to betray him.

"Eli did seem troubled," I say, "but so do many of my students. They go through a lot." And though this is true, it's true in the way that it simply reaches out toward the unknowable—in a way that all dark roads can look familiar, even when they aren't. I will regret it once the day is over, when Eddie and I walk past the protesters dressed as angels, start drinking at the hotel across the street. And for the rest of my life, I will wonder what Susan saw that made her think I'd admit the truth. I will regret that she was wrong.

When it's Susan's turn to call her witnesses, she starts with a cognitive scientist who explains that teenage brains are impulsive. She gets Dr. Schlessinger to talk about your auditory hallucinations, admit that the shooting was symptomatic of a mental illness. She asks Joe: Do you consider Eli to be a member of your family? She asks Mr. Madsen: Did you know him to be mean-spirited?

Then she calls your father. It's the only time you've ever seen him in a tie, as well as professorial eyeglasses, his hair cut short on the sides and combed on the top. For all the jurors know, this is what he looks like all the time. They can't picture him snarling in the mirror, calling himself a yuppie. They don't realize how desperate he must be.

Susan begins by asking him how many times he's been able to visit, how many days he's spent in court. She asks: "Why is it important for you to be in the room with Eli?"

"I don't know if this makes sense," he says, "but the person before me is neither the one who did it, nor the one who didn't, nor the one who is innocent." Your father's voice cracks, then he steadies himself. "If anyone should take responsibility for this, it's me. After my wife died, I thought I knew what hardship was. I didn't realize it's a cycle with no beginning. That it was some large, harmless-looking spiral that incrementally tightened. That it darkened to a pit. Became the thing that swallowed us."

"Where did this darkness come from, Mr. Habberton?"

"I don't know—everywhere, I suppose."

"Do you still love your son?

He nods solemnly. "You can't let your child's worst choices define them."

When your father leaves the stand, you consider, for perhaps the first time, that after all this, he will be the one who has to bury you. Without you, he will have nothing left of the family he had built. Those dinners the two of you ate in front of the television, egg sandwiches or tavern pizza, waiting for your mother to come back from the night shift—sometimes going to bed without her, but being able to wake up and know, just by the way the house felt, whether or not she had come home. For a moment, you return to hearing her voice, which is outside time, unique and abundant as an element. "Eli," she says, "are you still disappointed in me?"

———

At the end of the trial, Susan explains how your lifetime in prison would be worse than death. The prosecutor quotes Emerson, saying: "The only person you are destined to become is the one you decide to be." The jury deliberates for three days, and when they come back, the forewoman reads a statement saying all seventeen of them agree you should die. They say the mitigating factors do not outweigh the horror of your crime. That you do not understand the preciousness of life. If there ever was a case that should call for the maximum sentence, they say, this is the one.

When the judge states you will be put to death in the manner prescribed by the law, almost everyone in the courtroom cheers. You hear it the way a siren can fill an entire city. You tell yourself that while it's the sound of everyone hating you, misunderstanding you, and buying into the same collective delusion, it's also the sound of the world fearing and striking back at you. It is also your last chance at beauty—the sound that will enshrine you.

The officer who drives you to Feliciana State Prison talks like some kind of mordant tour operator. He explains how, until very recently, it was named after a West African slave port. Its prisoners toiled in cotton fields, supervised by police on horseback. Now, he says, it has a garment factory that makes clothes for JC Penney. He says there is a dome built around the rectangular structure of cells, which means you could escape from one building and still be trapped in another. The only man who ever managed to jump the fence and beat the dogs stole a fisherman's truck, then crashed into a swamp and drowned.

While he talks, you watch the landscape beyond the heavily tinted van windows. It is the kind of bright, mad day when the sun at your back puts everything into sharp focus. First, you drive through Eudora and Blytheville. You pass a number of old men selling flags in gas station parking lots. A discount grocery store likely stocked with shelves of expired fruit cocktail. Soon, it's just auto body shops and trees dripping with Spanish moss. Collapsed wooden houses. Eventually, you're in the middle of a forest, tracing a pillar of strange smoke that's unfurling over the denuded trees. A razor-wire perimeter. Octagonal gun towers.

After processing, an entire riot team escorts you through the building, past tiers of cells on a metal catwalk. Some prisoners yell at you or stick small mirrors through the bars to watch. Others ignore you completely. They are kneeling before paintings of Jesus or talking back to their small televisions. They are hanging up socks or washing T-shirts in their toilets. Farther back, the vast aisle of cells shrinks into the double-tiered chamber of death row.

The first day in your cell, you return to your old ways of passing time. In the wall, you find a portrait that seems to follow you with its eyes. You listen to the other prisoners yelling at you, but you don't respond. You find mosquito larvae in the toilet. Smell the recirculated farts. You watch your own spectral image in a piece of gray-making metal that's supposed to serve as a mirror.

But when your twenty-three hours of solitary are up, and it's time for recreation, they don't put you in a sunlit room by yourself. They actually take you outside into the open air. They put you in a large dirt-floor cage that's coiled with concertina wire. A few dumbbells sit beneath a basketball hoop made from a milk crate. On the other side there's another, much bigger cage, with a concrete terrace that overlooks a bocce ball court. A television under a plywood roof plays *Xena: Warrior Princess*, and there's another inmate, watching with his back turned. He doesn't see you at first, so you go into the corner and pick up the basketball, but you don't shoot, just squeeze it in your palms like it's a balloon you're trying to pop.

"Hey!" says the guy in the other cage. "Young man! Hello there!"

At first, you consider responding. He's yelling at you in a friendly manner, with little inflection, but you're not sure why he wants your attention. He's wearing shorts, rhino boots, and his torso is bulging and hardened in a way that tells you he hasn't seen the free world since before you were born. What could you two possibly have to say to each other? You stay in the far corner of the cage, clutching the basketball until your hour is finished, dismissing him as some kind of lifetime criminal who belongs here, and who thus deserves society's collective scorn—a label that, for whatever reason, you do not ascribe to yourself.

This goes on for about a week. Every time you're let outside, this guy is there, trying to get your attention. He says his name is Ray. You continue to ignore him, but while you do, your reality begins to atrophy. You don't recognize your own voice. You have no money to buy candy or books from the commissary because you spent what little you had on cheap headphones to plug into a jack in the wall, which only plays Spanish radio or rhythm and blues. You spend your days wrapped in a blanket, staring at the wall.

Eventually, you give up. You don't care if he's luring you to the fence so he can stab you with a sharpened chicken bone or run his hand menacingly across his throat. You're tired. You need something to happen.

"What took you so long?" he says.

"Didn't feel like talking."

"I understand that." He looks past you, puts his hand over his eyes to block the sun, reading the landscape, looking down toward the sunken railway corridor at your back.

"So, how are you?" you ask.

"Me?" he says, somewhat indignantly. "I'm blessed. Been begging the COs forever to put two people up in here at once. Didn't think they'd give me some kid, though."

"I'm not a kid."

He laughs, rolling back on his heels. "In here, people are going to treat you how you carry yourself. And you've been carrying yourself like a kid, I'm sorry to say."

You consider insulting him back, or walking away, but you're too desperate. At this point, making eye contact is something you haven't done in weeks. Doing so feels like an entire conversation.

This is how you make a friend. You let him do all the talking, which means you will never have to dismantle yourself before another person. He tells you about living in Houston, sleeping under parked cars, alleys lit with dumpster fires. He says he's been on the row for fifteen years, used to fight all the time because he yearned for physical contact with the riot team. He's in here because his friend botched a robbery, shot a shopkeeper in the arm, but the bullet ricocheted off his elbow and into his heart. Says something about a plea deal, how his lawyers are still looking for exculpatory evidence. He rants about racist pardon board members, and when you allude to Susan's plan to rehumanize you, he erupts in laughter. "How do you think a system that's structured to erase you is going to rehumanize you?" he asks.

At times, talking to Ray makes you miss Gordon. You want to be back in that house, sinking into a beanbag chair, listening to him explain how FEMA is building concentration camps, how artificial sweetener might be controlling our thoughts.

Your life solidifies a little. You are a productive reader, become neat and fastidious, cleaning the flagstone floors of your cell with a toothbrush. Your disciplinary write-ups cease. You get in bed once your neighbor turns off the ten o'clock news. You realize you can see Ray's cell down the hall if you look from the right angle, so the two of you put socks on your hands, develop a sort of sock-semaphore communication system and start a Belgian waffle smuggling ring you coordinate with one of the cooks, who puts leftovers into latex gloves.

Your father visits occasionally. In the beginning he doesn't look exhausted from the long drive, or from waiting long hours in the visitor center without food. He talks about the appeals process, which he has calculated will last for the next twelve years. Something about a nationwide shortage of sodium thiopental. He says he's been going to church with Joe. Says he's met with some of the victims' families and they've forgiven you. He talks about your life with a vision that is more vivid than how you view it. Sometimes, you wonder if he needs this more than you do.

Months that feel like years go by, and summer wakes into the sky. You start to resent the daylight. How gluttonous and loud it is. You miss the dark, the light that is left upon the earth. The way clouds marble the sky. The trees thrusting nightward in mysterious shapes. You receive letters from angry strangers or pastors trying to save your soul. You look for Gordon's signature at the bottom of every one, always feeling a mix of relief and disappointment when it isn't him. When you write back, you must do so on an old typewriter that holds the paper crooked, which you only get access to one hour a week.

Then one day, Ray is late to recreation, and when he gets there, he kneels before the fence in the fetid dirt, like he's bracing himself before a strong wind.

"Fifth Circuit Court," he says, "rejected it out of hand."

You're still confused by the complexity of the appeals process, habeas proceedings, the pardon board hearings and letters to governors, but it's Ray's delivery that tells you how finished he is. You know he's been to the death chamber once before, only to be called back after they couldn't get the drug in time. He told you about it once: how he wrote his own obituary, mailed goodbye cards to everyone he knew. How the associate wardens had already arrived with their walkie-talkies. How a team of guards had already put a diaper on him, just before the phone rang.

Now he is telling you again. He gets hung up on how the state buries unclaimed bodies in metal caskets. How the funerals, so far out here in the middle of a national forest, are sparsely attended.

"Do you have someone coming to get your body?" you ask.

"Ain't gonna be no body," he says. He holds some dirt in his hands, dumps it on the front of his boot. "Let me ask you something, Eli—are you religious?"

"I'm in here for murder," you reply.

"That's not what I asked."

You shrug.

"Don't want to have a title on your back," he says. "I respect that."

"What about you?"

"I don't see any burning bushes, if that's what you mean. But I have been meeting with this pastoral counselor. Strange dude, always wearing these green suits. I was telling him how I was going to stop eating and refuse visitors. How I'm not going to leave quietly. How I'm innocent. All he said in response was that I have the freedom to choose whether I die with hate or love in my heart."

It's almost dark now, and the way he smirks into the orange prison floodlights make it seem like he's choosing love.

This is when you nod, even though, deep down, you think the price of love is a loss of wholeness. You think that, if people label you a monster, you might as well become a reflection of their misunderstanding.

You know when it's time for Ray to be moved to a holding cell in the death chamber because you hear the riot squad marching down the catwalk between the cells. His door rolls open. You overhear the thick rustle of leather boots and flak jackets, voices shouting over gas masks. Stop resisting! Grab his feet! Watch his head! Get the leg restraints! A body smacks against the wall. Leg irons scrape over the concrete. A canister of gas explodes from a gun, and it sounds like a glass ball bouncing in a cage. Then it's quiet, except for a series of small, pitiful gasps. The gas makes you choke and cough. As the tears and snot start rolling off your face, you tell yourself you're stupid for ever expecting anything different. This is what life does. It reneges on everything it gives.

The next time you're let out for recreation, there's no one else in the yard, just some quiet sparrows perched on the wire and a swarm of hard, blind bugs so thick they could carry you away. You feel your emotional world shrinking into nothing. You think that maybe this entire time, you were never really human. Other people were always occupying you, and now that no one is around, you are no longer a man, but a domino waiting to be flicked. A snake that keeps biting after getting decapitated. A ghost modulating in light.

A year goes by, and your father keeps visiting, but he starts looking chalky, loses all his ruddiness, skin taut on his cheekbones as if from starvation. He loses interest in your conversations even before the hour is up, so you find yourself trying to move them along. Dad, you say, do you remember our backyard? Do you remember the hot dog stand outside the hardware store? Those days we spent balancing on deck joists? Do you remember that time I decided to quit football because it was snowing? How we sat in the car, watching everyone chase each other around as the lines of the field disappeared?

This works for a short while, but relationships are maintained by creating new memories, not by recasting old ones. Even before you run out of stories, your father begins to retreat. You get the sense he does not want to go back to those places. In each of them, there seems to be a trace of what you became. Eventually, even he becomes something you have to imagine rather than experience. You wake up and picture him driving toward a rental house, sun still climbing the hills. You think about him kneeling on the floor, wearing a back brace and a sweat-sullied bandana, snapping planks of laminate floor together. You imagine him pissing into Gatorade bottles. Cooking Hungry-Man Dinners in the microwave he carries to every jobsite. You hear him teaching you how to install tile. "Good times," he says, in that idiosyncratic way of his, as he smoothes your section with a grout float, like it's a painting he's pleased to wipe away.

He visits twice one year, then only once. Susan doesn't answer her phone, just sends you postcards whenever she's on vacation. You tell yourself this is a good thing, because every time you start to hope, it's like planting a tiny tree that someone's just going to mulch in the morning. Your life becomes an empty cul-de-sac. A shipworm hole in a boat. There are days when you can't talk or get out of bed. Then you realize that if you don't recover, you might die before they put you to death.

At one point, you actually convince yourself you've died. You wake up suddenly in the night. The world is shrouded in darkness, but your cell door has been opened, and beyond it there's a light. It's not a vague light—it almost looks like an envelope on fire, suspended in the air, cutting deep gashes into the darkness. You know it is a letter from Gordon. You approach your cell door, reaching after it. A mess of words flicker inside. You want to read them, but the envelope swings away, out of sight, until it comes hurling toward you, crashing into your cell, scattering flames across the floor. You try to stomp it out, but it's filled with fluid that splashes all over your legs, then combusts, and that's how you die: wrapped in your wool blanket, rolling on the floor, hoping the flames are taking you to the end of another nightmare.

Another day comes. You remember seeing a wad of paper on fire. You remember shutting your cell door, cleaning ash off your floor, then flushing it down the toilet. Like many things at this point in your life, you are so alone in this moment that you can't know if it's really happening. You find scorch marks on the tile. You sleep with burned scraps of paper under your pillow. But at a certain point, even those mementos don't convince you of anything. Death has become a porous border, a short, empty tunnel you enter at the same moment you are leaving.

YOUNG FATHERS

EDDIE

You are jogging down the empty ramp of a campus parking deck when your phone rings. At first, you don't think it's for you because the sound is coming toward you, echoing off the precast concrete and filling the air with possibility, the way a single church bell can pervade an entire city. But when you answer, it's Jean—Casey's mother. She says the Dean just called and told her about the "terrible accident" on campus, which is a phrase that even now seems oddly hopeful. You tell her you are aware of this accident. In fact, you tried running to the barricaded library, and now you're getting Casey's car so you can drive to the hospital—which has gone code black, keeps putting you on hold—so you can find her. You're not even done explaining your plan before Casey's mom tells you to stop. "Your proper place during this crisis," she says, "is at home, not running around a crime scene in your pajamas, showing up to hospitals and trying to pull a body out of a murder investigation."

This is the first time you're told that Casey is dead, and though you do not accept its logic, you follow Jean's command. You find Casey's car on the top deck, from which you can see sirens on the opposite side of campus lighting up the frosty rooftops. You start driving down MLK, past the mass grave of dollar stores, under the even clouds converging like one stoic slab of ice. At this point, you decide that Casey's death is something that happened, but only on campus.

It did not happen at home, for example, where you can picture her so clearly. You imagine her sitting at the dining table as you enter, protesting a smile as light torpedoes down from the chandelier toward her face, like a B-movie actress who just teleported back from her home planet. You can see her closing her laptop, standing to explain everything. You can't wait to hear what she has to say.

But when you arrive, your house looks defective. Beyond the ligatures of redbuds and mulberry trees, the dark windows hang agog like leaden caves. The brick pillars on the porch have a worrying tilt, and the long hypotenuse of the sheet metal roof floats into the remoteness of the sky. When you open the door, the house is filled with emphatic silence. The kitchen table is strewn with old coupon books and credit card mailers. The ceiling fan is on, silently rotating the pots of philodendrons hanging from the rough-cut rafters. Out of blind habit, you open the fridge and find a half-eaten apple. On the couch, a hair in a bicycle helmet. You kneel down next to the plastic Christmas tree in the corner, cataloging all the presents. The Aztec-print throw blanket you bought, the surrealist painting of an elk, and the large misshapen present with your name on it, wrapped in gold ribbon. As you peer at each item, you can't decide whether it is a link to her potential recovery, or death confirming itself.

The entire night does not budge, doesn't let you inside of it, and then spits you out into the pit of the morning. The doorbell rings, and Casey's parents are standing there. You barely see them at first. You look beyond them to their parked car, as if expecting to catch a face in the window, but there's nothing. Just the empty cab of their rusted Suburban and fog retiring up the side of the mountain.

They come in and sit down, and for a long time you're just alone together, watching the wild and distracted looks on each other's faces. Eventually, your own parents show up, then Casey's sister, her husband Robert, and then me. Someone throws together a pot of soup filled with chopped yams and onion, topped with wilted parsley we find in the fridge. We eat it out of paper bowls that appear from no-where. We make phone calls, and that's when the story breaks on the news. A picture of Eli appears, one that's clearly lifted from a social media account. In it, he's sitting on a plaid couch in a cluttered room wearing a black T-shirt, his mouth hanging open like he's in a Green Day music video.

"Shit," I say. The word takes a moment to enter the room, and then it blisters open. "I know him."

Everyone turns to me. I explain meeting with Eli in my office, because at first it seems like a story that will reveal something im-portant, like the tragedy is already circling around to explain itself. But when I finish, all that's been confirmed is that I was there. That I had a chance to put my hand between the falling dominoes and, for whatever reason, I didn't.

I wait as everyone takes a moment to feel through the story, to march around its empty cul-de-sac. The room turns bright as I wait for some kind of response or verdict. I close my eyes, but there is no darkness, just the spectral image of Eli in my office. His thick, sandy hair. The map of dirt on his pants. The future that is now disgorging from him.

"You did nothing wrong," you say. You have turned to face me, but you're looking beyond the frame of my eyes. "Even if you did, there's no room left in this world to feel guilty."

What you mean by this, I'm not sure. At first, I think you're as-signing all this used-up guilt to Eli, or maybe to yourself. But then I think you're just talking about guilt like it's some continuous sub-stance that's already moved into every crevice of our lives.

Later, aerial cameras follow portable morgues as they leave cam-pus at dawn. Casey's sister sweeps the entire house, finding large food scraps and dried-up bugs in neglected corners. Her dad flips through the books on your coffee table dotted with marginalia. You go out-side alone to smoke a cigarette, and a semi truck rumbles by from the dairy processing plant down the street. Two children are displayed on its side, and for a moment you are filled with resentment toward them, the way they smile and hold their milk glasses over their heads in triumph. And when the truck disappears, you attempt again to experience Casey's absence, but you can't. She is the sun you just stepped out of for a second. You are still aware of its warmth, still able to see it spreading across the Ozarka skyline, encasing everyone in the same abrogating light.

For several days, you wait for some kind of phone call or report that maps out the hard facts preceding Casey's death. But the only person who contacts you is an officer who explains the gun Eli used, clarifies that Casey was "a target of opportunity." Meanwhile, the public spectacle of her death marches on, and each day you step farther out of the plot of your own life and into the larger narrative in which everyone is disappearing. Musical preludes pour into churchyards. University taskforces assemble, send out colored spreadsheets of upcoming funerals and vigils. There are reflection gatherings in sports arenas. Talks of senate judiciary committees, epidemiological paths of gun violence, troubled youths. Among the many things given to you is a care package from Virginia Tech. In it, a brochure says to remember that death is one of the greatest puzzles of human existence. "Rather than explaining it away," it says, "try to embrace the mystery," which to you sounds like the kind of language that belongs in a bad art class. You think: How do you experience darkness by choosing to live inside it? What's the point in deciding that everyone is trapped in the same oarless boat?

Amidst all this, you find yourself actually looking forward to Casey's memorial and funeral. You want to enter a place where her death will not be universalized. You imagine standing in the fractured light of a leaded window and feeling her vast incompleteness. You imagine your oval shadow spreading across her body. But when those moments actually come, you're staring down an aisle of strangers holding programs, tucking little pictures of Casey inside their wallets like morbid trading cards. You're giving hugs, feigning stoicism. You say, "That's what a tragedy is, I suppose," without really wanting to. And when you see her, you realize a dead body can only capture someone as completely as an uncanny photograph. That unchanging face, those unseeing eyes. It isn't her, you think, as you look at her. A body is not a person. And when you cry, it's not because you feel the loss, but because you don't. You try to tell yourself what you are feeling is grief—that this denial and emptiness is part of the process—but it never really feels like grief. It feels like something else entirely. Something more like suspense.

Eventually, you decide you want to be alone, because while togetherness has sheltered you from limitless anger, kept you alive and fed you, it has also skimmed you across the surface of your pain. And you're worried that, as this pain becomes less raw, so will your memories. So you tell everyone to leave, start digging through Casey's things, and find a stack of cassette tapes she bought at local shows. You play them on the stereo, which you turn all the way up and stand before wearing her bathrobe, a space heater between your legs. You wrap yourself in the membrane of brute-force punk catharsis, the disembodied menace of vocals, the big tent guitar solos. Then you start hearing something disarmingly gentle behind it all. There are slurred notes from barrelhouse pianos, lonely yelps in basement chorus lines. You can see Casey listening to this in the Riot Room, standing in the back beside the walk-up window that used to sell slices of pizza but is now just a rack of chips and tobacco products. She smokes on the back deck overlooking the gravel parking lot, then walks home, stopping by the karaoke bar, ordering a gin and soda with olive juice, singing "Heart of Gold" in her best Linda Ronstadt contralto. Then she comes through the front door, her ears ringing the same way yours are now, blocking out a frequency you will never hear again.

This is how you develop strange fealties to objects of loss. You read the passages she underlined in all her books, water and fertilize all the plants in the house, organize her underwear drawer. Christmas is long gone, so you open the big misshapen present with your name on it and uncover a microfiber dog bed with an insertable tufted pillow. It seems like a mistake at first, until you realize it must be for a dog she was planning to adopt. You look through her browsing history, call local shelters, sift through wanted ads, asking people if someone named Casey Bishop contacted them about a dog, but no one knows anything. You're certain this unfinished act contains some message about a potential child. Is the dog a replacement for one? A companion? A test run? In the end, you conclude that it was just something you both wanted. You have to account for the fact that sometimes, things really are that simple.

January strays into a new year, and before classes start, the university offers you a semester-long paid sabbatical, which is unprecedented for a second-year adjunct who previously made $2,000 per class with no health benefits and no job security. You take it, and during this time I visit your house often, trying my best just to be alone with you. We play cards, walk down to the pool hall, watch documentaries about space travel. At one point, you relay the story to me about the dog bed, and I offer to go get one with you. You say this is not something you're ready for, but then the next day we're at the animal shelter. A volunteer takes us into the living quarters, and we walk by the poorly welded bars until you kneel before a dog named "Butternut." She has a long, beefy torso, small legs, and a brindle coat. Her pointy, Yoda-like ears lay back guiltily as she greets us, peeing on the concrete a little. She's probably the ugliest dog we've seen, but there's a vast whiteness around her large blue eyes, which have a human complexity to them. So you adopt her, rename her "Allie," pay for a $2,500 heartworm treatment with part of your victim restitution money, and it's not long before we're all driving back across town. It's one of those unthawing pre-spring days where you can feel the sun entering the new buds of trees and releasing warmth into the ground below. We go out for fast food, and you're passing a ketchup packet to me when Allie lunges forward, snatching it out of your hands, swallowing the whole thing. It's funny, the way she returns to looking so gentle and oafish after biting something out of your hand, so we laugh, and we don't stop. We laugh for so long that we step outside the confines of our lives for a moment, and we keep laughing not because it's still funny, but because it's a state from which we are afraid to return.

Several weeks later, you call and ask me to come over and help you sort through Casey's clothes. It's an endeavor I secretly doubt you're ready for, and I guess I'm correct, because while I'm on my way over, you're examining a pair of her jeans and find a folded diagram that your counselor drew back when you were in couples therapy. Suddenly, you're sitting in his office with Casey as he swings his fountain pen across a notepad, drawing an infinity symbol that maps how innocent actions trigger thoughts related to attachment fears, feed defensive responses, then over time become cyclical patterns of rejection and escalation. "Think of it this way," he says, crossing his legs and revealing his Christmas tree socks. "You two are in a tennis match and all you're focused on are a few volleys. You're not seeing the game itself. In fact, you don't even know you're playing tennis." At this point, you look at Casey, who is sitting with her back toward the window. Sun blares through it, casting a coppery light on everything in the room. The white noise machine in the hallway hisses, like an ocean is about to pour into your field of vision, and you start having one of those moments where you grasp the depth of an illusion. You can see the dead-end pattern of mutual blame that is consuming your marriage, and you can see the way out of it.

So when I finally arrive, the bags that were supposed to be filled with Casey's clothes are now filled with yours. You say you can't be in this house anymore, because here the past years of your marriage lie in a queue ahead of you. And you can't be in this town, either. People here are trying to move on, and you're starting to resent them for it. "I'm in a spiral that's neither going up, nor down," you say, and as we hug goodbye, I can almost feel the different brands of grief that will creep through the back door when you leave. It will be a long time before we see each other again.

Several years before, your parents moved out of your childhood home to a neighborhood on the outskirts of Little Rock called Chanel Valley, a foreign-branded sprawl of gated communities built en masse in the early 2000s. To get there, you drive past large agricultural lots and wooded areas that haven't been rezoned or clear-cut, then pull up to the iron swing gate of Marin Estates. A security guard in a booth nods as you enter the passcode into a keypad, which sits beneath the nebulous mural of a lighthouse. You already feel out of place, driving slow in Casey's sun-bleached Nissan, a gremlin-faced dog sniffing out the window. Without ever seeing anyone, you bet the median age is around fifty-five. You can feel it in the top-notch landscaping, swirls of bark mulch, lacy drapes, and the bewildering mix of faux stucco, brick facades, and imbalanced Palladian windows. You almost forget why you came here until your parents let you inside, where no particularly strong memory of Casey bears down on you. Here, it's just healthy fichus plants, beach resort furniture, and digital photo frames that scroll through pictures of weddings and hunting trips you didn't attend. The history within this house is short and sterile, and therefore free of unprocessed memories.

In the mornings, your parents go to work and you stay at home like a sick child. You make coffee with their high-tech single-serving beverage pod and sit on the sectional leather sofa, your bare feet massaging the carpet that's more padded than a wrestling mat. You walk Allie on sidewalks so white that spitting on them seems like a chargeable offense. You take long showers, exercise on the elliptical in the garage, squeezing every small pleasure out of the house until your life is one of those dreams where nothing bad happens, but the whole atmosphere is grim and deadly. You wake up beneath neurotically busy wallpaper, surrounded by tall dressers that look like they're staging an arrest. You try to watch TV, but all you find are CSI episodes that gaslight rape victims, SNL skits where straight actors play sassy gay princes, and an adult cartoon about a Mexican boxer named "El Pollo Creed." And when your father comes home, he keeps bending down to pet Allie, but something in his smell and posture makes her pee on the carpet. He gets angry every time, which reinforces her submissive behavior. You think: how could someone raise a child and not understand this? You try seeking out your mother for commiseration, but she just plays the diplomat, speaks about your father with the kind of reverence typically reserved for dead people. Eventually, you start looking forward to the night, when the house feels partially yours again. You get out of bed and eat cereal standing in the kitchen, under the dim glow of unfamiliar electronics, waiting to feel your soul and your body at the same time again. You walk back down the hallway and believe, if only for a second, that Casey is in the room you're groping toward.

Then one day, you check the news on your phone and learn that Eli has been deemed competent to stand trial. All it takes is a quick look at the headlines to see the whole debate regarding the death penalty has been reignited. Once again, people are talking about evil like it's a religion everyone believes in. They are saying Eli was born with a unique capacity for violence that just flicked on, like a creature galvanized by lightning. They are saying ORDER THE DRUGS NOW and TALL TREE SHORT ROPE. You try to put your phone away, but it's too late. You pace the empty house, trying to imagine how Eli's death would make you feel, but it's like boarding a too-fast carousel that keeps throwing you to the ground. At one point you stop and involuntarily shout, "Dr. Barrabus Hughes!" You have no idea where you got this name until you find a coffee cup on the counter advertising a local dentist. This is how people go crazy, you think.

So you go on a walk to clear your head, which makes you feel better until you approach the edge of a semicircular driveway, where an Ozarka Racoons flag hangs on a commercial-grade flagpole, dead in the air at half mast. It has been three months since the shooting, and everywhere you go, there's still some stranger who wants to carry the ghost of your wife, and the eleven people who died with her, on his shoulders. You think: if they want to pretend like they lost someone in that library, they might as well pretend they were the one who blasted it with bullets, too. You stand there for a long time, glaring at the obese rotunda that protrudes from the house, the giant white columns, and the windows beyond them reflecting some untraceable part of the sky. Ultimately, you wonder why you're directing anger toward this house, and people inside it, and not Eli. It's like the collective response to the shooting has become indistinguishable from the shooting itself.

Later that night, you sit down for dinner and your father clears his throat and prays about unending grace and servitude like he usually does. "And we pray for your justice, oh Lord," he adds, "for it to come quick and to be served against the wicked."

"I think the word you're looking for is vengeance," you interrupt.

Your father opens his eyes and looks at you, but does not unclasp his hands. "That's not what I meant."

At this point, you realize that interjecting was a mistake, that you had a bad day and now you're seeking understanding from the person least likely to give it. But it's too late. "I just think it's quite the coincidence," you say, "that of all days, today is when you start praying for justice."

Your father turns to your mother, as if to signal that he's exercising caution, like he doesn't want to have to spell things out for you.

"I don't know what will happen to Eli," he says, "but I think we're all struggling to find the correct response. And the thing is—we have to respond. We have to ask ourselves, what kind of fate does someone like that deserve? What kind of person would kill for something they wouldn't also die for?"

The beauty in your father's response is that it allows him to defend the side he's on without actually taking it. Now, if you keep arguing, you'll be fighting for a leverage that does not exist. You do it anyway. You try to explain how pointless it is to believe in evil if it's something we are always separating ourselves from. "Do you realize how shortsighted and hypocritical it is to appeal to Eli's moral conscience by killing him?"

But all your father has to do is throw his hands up. "Eddie," he says, "that's not what I was talking about." He speaks in that tone of faux gentility he uses to cast you as an aggressor. "For me, God's Justice is a light switch in a dark room that we're fumbling toward," he says, transitioning right into that "God is a fixed point of reference" speech, and there you are, just eating the balsamic-glazed pork tenderloin and listening. If you try to interrupt now and say that Eli's sentence has nothing to do with God, he would bring in his finish move. He would go full persecution complex on your ass. "It's fine if you don't believe in God," he would say, "but I don't appreciate how you constantly attack me for it."

Whenever your father carries on about God like this, you typically accept the stalemate and wait to move on. But sometimes, it taps into a sentimental longing, reminiscent of your childhood, when you listened to the same speeches and did not question their legitimacy. After all, God is what you passed through to get where you are now, and perhaps this means you can never really stop believing in it. What if, for example, this whole time God was just surrounding you like negative space in a painting? What if you've been experiencing it as a void rather than an entity? This is what you feel now, as your father explains how our own depravity makes God look evil to us. You follow him along that descending ladder, to a place where God falls down like snow on the entire argument, erasing all the lines that boxed you out of His grace. For a moment, you do not seek wisdom beyond God because God is the ineffable itself.

At first, you think this is a dismissible episode. But when you go to sleep and wake up the next day, that same thought is waiting for you. God as a flat region. God as a changing form, like a cliff avalanching into a valley. So you decide to confront God. You pray, but there's too much noise in your head. You read scripture, but every passage feels empty and arcane. You open up the Bible at random and it says, "Don't concern yourself with things that are too wonderful," then, "Taketh and dasheth thy little ones against the stones."

So one Sunday in April, you agree to go to church with your parents. You think this is where you can confront the God of your childhood, but when you arrive, it's one of those new non-denominational exurban churches that look like a corporate headquarters-slash-junior college. Inside, there's a cappuccino cart, a Butler Chicken, and all the young men are wearing those daddy's-got-oil-money blue plaid blazers. The sermon is delivered in a sprawling auditorium, where a young pastor wearing a designer hunting vest jokes about vegetarians and football and explains how the liberal zeitgeist "tests our faith." Father this, father that he says, invoking God like he's some hip young dad whose emotional distance is supposed to be valuable and reassuring. This, you think, is just the God you came to know later in life, with all its predictable gloss.

So next Sunday, you relocate to the church you frequented as a child. To get there, you drive through a mixed-used area of eastern Little Rock and park beside a Laundromat. The church is exactly how you remember it, with buff blockwork and a cedar-plank roof that evokes both a local gym and a barn. You walk inside and sit in the back, beneath an organ loft, staring at the altar, which is just a thin cross surrounded by artificial flowers. Eventually, a musical prelude begins, and the pastor takes the stage. He wears a stole and cincture, preaches about the parable of the dishonest steward. You close your eyes, trying to feel God as you once did. But it's not the same here, ten years later. Now, you stare at the coffin-sized windows thinking about how poorly attended the service is. Compared to your parents' congregation, it feels like some Christian island of misfit toys. So after the next hymn, during the hesitant applause, you tell yourself this episode is over.

You slip out the back door, drive through the streetcar suburbs, get on the freeway that stretches out toward the fracklands. Out here, you should feel relieved, but you don't. You're crying. You tell yourself you can't be separate from God, because God is just a comfortable bedtime story. It doesn't work. You keep hoping that your faith will return, because if God isn't out there waiting in the beyond, then you have to assume that Casey isn't, either. Disbelieving feels like losing her all over again.

You've always felt that the moment you realize it's summer is also the moment you sense it's coming to an end. Somehow, you overlook those first days when the sun lopes back into the sky and the air is shredded with cicadas. All of a sudden, entire roadsides bloom with lupine and patio bars crowd with smokers, dogs, and cover bands playing "Mustang Sally." When this happens, you're still at your parents' house. You're trying to read for the upcoming semester, but there are still so many noises and twisted faces on each page, in between the words. You're trying to write, but your half-finished novel, in which "a family confronts long-buried secrets and struggles for redemption," has lost its meaning entirely. You sleep and watch TV. Each day feels like one warped board getting nailed to another. Then Jean calls. It's a quick exchange, in which she suggests you come visit the farm, and when you ask if tomorrow is good, she cackles. "We've got no plans to leave," she says, which immediately conjures their insular house and the bald landscape around it, like a crater in the unincorporated forest.

At first, you think you're just going for dinner. You leave in the morning, drive all the way back up into the mountains, where you remember to pass the feed store, the antique shop, then take a left onto the dirt road just past the homemade sign advertising LUMPY'S DEAD ANIMAL SERVICE. You decide to honor Casey's memory by driving as fast as she used to. You bounce through potholes the size of cars, beside cliffs that drop off into cow pastures, beyond which sit (according to her) entire communities of trailers connected by ATV trails and hidden trash piles of baby diapers. You speed past an old barn, perched where it was dragged decades ago, resting on the fir poles used for skids. You dodge a pole of rebar demarcating an eroded cliff.

"What happens when you meet another car on this road?" you asked Casey, that first day she drove you out here.

"You don't," she said, shifting gears and lowering her chin.

Eventually, you pull up to her house, which is no longer her house, just the faded pink vinyl double-wide where Jean and Alan live. And when they greet you on the porch, stepping on the tall grass that's poking through the planks, you realize that leaving Marin Estates wasn't as traumatic as you thought. On the drive over here, you somehow succeeded in passing through a memory instead of jumping to the bottom of it.

At dinner, the three of you discuss farming systems and short stories. Unlike your parents, Jean and Alan inquire about the writing process rather than your accomplishments, which causes you to self-actualize as an artist for a bit. You forget that you're an underpaid adjunct whose only publication is in a now-defunct airline magazine. You find yourself saying things like, "I find my own cloud of unknowing and proceed through it."

"Nano from the get-go," says Alan, in a tone that makes it clear he's parroting the phrase from somewhere.

"What?"

"You have to recognize *nano from the get-go*," he says. "*Delta Orion* was Casey's favorite show as a kid."

"I have no idea what you're talking about."

"Are you kidding me?" He gets up from the dinner table and starts digging through a shelf of old VHS tapes. He laments he can only find the third season, but loads it into the VCR anyway. The show is a BBC sitcom from the nineties, which is an odd pastiche of science fiction, hijinks, and heartstring-tugging. It turns out that the phrase is from a talking-horse hologram who constantly tries to warn the captain of a nanorobot takeover, repeating it so often that he truncates it to "from the get-go." That's when the sound folds into Casey's voice. For the longest time, you just thought it was one of her hokey verbal tics. You remember that once, in the middle of an argument, she said, "Your boundary has been my trigger from the get-go!" and the high-low register in the phrase caused you to double over laughing. You think about this until the episode ends. Aside from all the robot jokes and euphemisms, the show is designed to reassure: an odd group of hapless space travelers get marooned in an unfamiliar galaxy, and they manage to live entirely free of dread, danger, and anxiety. The only shot of what actually surrounds them appears during the credits, when their craft drifts through a sea of homogeneous stars, as if trapped in an old screen saver.

The next morning, you wake up on the sofa to find Jean cooking breakfast. She bakes a quiche with mustard greens, small fragrant onions, and fingerling potatoes. She makes a pot of cheap black coffee, red-eye gravy, and grits. When you finish eating, the room seems to have taken control of the mood, and you forego all your plans for the day. You don't leave. You follow Alan out behind the barn, where he shows you a foundation of cinderblocks in the soil that will be a new hydroponic greenhouse. He describes salad greens in A-frame shelves, substrates, and nutrients from fish waste, but when you try to imagine the greenhouse he's talking about, it seems too futuristic for the landscape that otherwise surrounds you, which looks like it was born wounded. The cords of stacked wood, wire hoops and worn row covers, jonquils wilting at the edge of the property. He hands you a shovel in the middle of a sentence, starts filling in the foundation blocks with dirt. All day, the blue sky falls down on you like a blanket. Allie stalks the barn cats, and Jean kneels in the upper garden of brassicas, interplanted with onions and garlic. And when the sun goes down, Alan sets up a work light that sears your shadow onto the dirt. You shovel cement until you're dizzy, then you eat tamales and watch *Delta Orion* until the couch engulfs you again. When you fall asleep, you dream of a flat darkness that defeats every word or thought.

Over the past six months, you've learned that if something feels good, you might as well lean into it as far as possible. You help Alan frame the greenhouse. You sit on a bucket in the garden rows and pull weeds from daikon radishes and squash. When it gets too hot, you take breaks to eat deer jerky and kimchi, drink flat beer. You take naps beside Allie, shaded in the amaranth, surrounded by bush crickets. You work harder than you need to, not wanting Jean or Alan to think you're some city boy who romanticizes the daily toil of their lives, who thinks its *cool* or *relaxing* to live apart from the captive economy he has bought into and to which he will no doubt return. So you don't tell them how refreshing it is to work outside, where each seasonal task has its own unique window of opportunity. How every dusk is unfamiliar because you're always waiting for it to open up. How the stars that gather into a broad moongate make you believe, at times, that there is no alternate future out there that has been stolen from you, the one you're still trying to get back.

But it's not long before you overestimate this inner peace. You start obsessing over Casey's old room, which you haven't been inside since that first year together. It's at the end of the hall behind a damaged hollow-core door, and since neither Jean nor Alan have shown it to you, you assume it's because they want to spare you the pain of revisiting whatever old clothes or yearbooks or juvenile band posters might be inside. But now, you feel ready to confront it. You wait until everyone is asleep, creep down the hallway past the bathroom, and turn the doorknob. Even before your eyes adjust, there's a deviance in the sharply etched shadows that fill the room. You turn on the light, and a broken futon frame leans against the wall. Beside it, an air conditioner covered in dust. Boxes of seeds. Books about homesteading. Car parts strewn across a twin mattress, half covered by a pink bedspread. You close the door, wondering what made you think that this room, the one you visited nearly six years ago, was something to which you could return. It makes you feel old, imagining how everything Casey left unfinished will disappear. You see yourself years from now, looking at pictures of her and realizing how young she was when she was murdered. How, as the years pass, she'll no longer look like someone who could be your wife, but a younger sister, or long-lost niece, or daughter.

It's time to go back to Ozarka. The semester is about to start, and you're out of homes to run away from. It's Sunday, so you decide to leave after helping Jean at the farmer's market. Together, you load up all the interlocking bins with vegetables, drive to downtown Blue Eye, and set up the canopy. You work the register, drinking coffee and eating deep-fried coconut balls, but all day everyone is talking about a storm that's supposed to come. The musicians leave, then the humane society volunteers, then some of the farmers pack up early. When the market is almost completely empty, you climb the hundred-foot fire observation tower at the edge of the parking lot to see if you can spot anything. The sky is mostly blue, except for a wall of clouds in the distance the color and consistency of pea soup. They reticulate a bit as they approach the back of a white Jesus statue that stands before an amphitheater in the distance, arms outstretched toward the small, aimless mountains.

You go back to the farm to cinch down garden row covers, tarp the unfinished greenhouse, and board up the windows. You help Alan let the goats out of the barn, then stand with him on the covered porch. It's hard to pin down, but something in his posture indicates he knows a storm isn't coming, but he feels good being prepared for it.

"What do we do now?" you say.

"We watch closely." He takes off his glasses to look into the distance. A valved hum of rain releases into the air. "Look," he says, pointing to a vinyl downspout. "I like to wait for the moment when the first rain comes rushing out of that elbow. Farthest it has shot is past that rock up there, by that piece of rebar."

The two of you wait for the water to come rushing, but it never does, despite the heavy rain. It's one of those moments when your perception of the moment enlarges, but you don't know why. You swear you can read the print on a Coke bottle resting in a ditch way down the road.

"Alan, can I ask you something?"

He nods.

"What do you really think about Eli getting the death penalty?"

"Most of the time," he says, "I think that's what he deserves."

To this statement, you have no follow-up. In fact, you feel like you understand how he feels. Killing Eli is just one of the many imperfect ways to prevent him from becoming the God he wanted to be. It is revenge, sure, but revenge is not supposed to be some accurate measurement of loss. It is accepting that life is something you can crush in your fist. That you can fuck people out of the hand that was dealt to them. That although the prank Eli played was cruel, it was also true. You understand this so fully you think maybe it's not Alan feeling it, but you.

You stay one last night on the farm, waiting for the storm. Before you go to sleep, Alan tells you to listen for a train barreling through a corridor toward the house. That's what a tornado sounds like, he says. So you lie there, cataloguing whatever noises seep through the silence. You don't hear much, so you concentrate. You think: Heavy rail tires. Ship containers filled with gravel. A long carriage accelerating down a hill. You try to focus on that type of noise, but when you jolt awake in a cold sweat, fearing for your life, the sound you keep imagining is unnatural and deliberate, like the howl of a siren.

When you return to campus, the first thing you learn is that the entire structure of the composition class you're teaching has been revamped. You do not learn this from a departmental meeting or email, but from another adjunct in the staff computer lab. Developing writing skills through analyzing literature, he says, no longer befits contemporary students at OU, who are job-focused, concerned about skyrocketing loan debt, and traumatized by the shooting. They can't be reading stories about toxic gas descending upon professors of Nazism studies, or Dominican immigrants being murdered by police, or delusional men swimming home through neighborhood pools. They can't read poems about "black hearts bleeding red," or graphic novels that delineate bipolar disorder. According to him, they should "learn how to navigate the technical language in their chosen fields of study." They should know pedagogical theory, data analysis, and "rhetorical situations." Their essays should answer questions like, "How are the goals and characteristics of your chosen major reflected in its discourse?"

For a few days, you tell yourself you have to quit, but you can't imagine an alternate future, other than sitting at home, writing bitter think-pieces about the slow meltdown of academia into corporatization. So you lower your head, prepare your syllabus, and when classes start, you develop a routine. You wake at sunrise to prepare for your first class at 9 a.m., teach through the afternoon, conduct office hours, and draw up lesson plans at Common Grounds, listening to hardcore punk through noise-canceling headphones to stay awake. You go home, pour whiskey into a tallboy, and grade papers until your marginal comments turn into surly acronyms and interrobangs. During this time, you don't have a lot of space to think about Casey. And when you do, you find yourself over-intellectualizing the matter in the affected style of the essays you're teaching. "The rhetorical situation of Tragedy," you write in your journal, "is one where the community feels like it owns the event. It must be disassociated from grief, which is a passive individual experience, and then from mourning, which is attentive."

But the teaching material isn't as valueless as you expected. As a class, you explore the performative aspects of writing, how academia reproduces repressive systems of cultural domination, then you apply these analytic tools when you teach the "One Community" book the whole college is supposed to read. In it, a white journalist digs into the life of a black woman whose cancer-resistant cells were stolen from her and sold for profit. It explores the history of racist medical practices in America, but does so with one of those underlying white-intellectual-savior narratives you can't ignore. You basically just hate-read the book with your students. You dissect how scared the journalist seems as she drives past empty row houses in St. Louis, then meets the family and patronizingly reads a bunch of jargon-filled medical documents to them. But you take it too far, end up turning her into an evil embodiment of racism. So then you have to backpedal, try to explain times when you have "stood up" for minorities in a way that just benefitted yourself. But you don't explain it well, and your students think you just accidentally admitted to being a bigot, rather than trying to implicate a culture that would allow this book to be championed. They sigh, give you disparaging looks, which you decide to do nothing about, since this ire is something you deserve.

Finals begin, and people start gathering for the anniversary of the shooting, sharing pictures and personal testimonies, their hymns and candles bouncing off the profusion of glass and metal of the new library. When this happens, you realize that this year, like all the ones ahead of it, will travel in a circle that leads back to Casey's death. Wanting to avoid this, you go see your counselor, who again reminds you that loss is not something you work to overcome—it's an absence that lives. "Only a fool would run through the rain to escape it," he says, which is true, but it's also advice you cannot hear.

By now, you're simply fed up with your loss. It's starting to seem like a selfish preoccupation. When you look back on the past year, you think of all the moments when you acted as if Casey's death mattered chiefly in its effect on you. What about her point of view? There are still large swaths of her life you don't understand, and the longer you mope around, pushing your memories out into the sea of your past and letting the tides have their way, the more likely she will become not herself, but something you constructed, a person who is suspended in your ego. So you decide not to accept your loss. Instead, you resolve to crawl out from under it.

So you finally write back to an EMT who sent you a letter after the shooting, telling you she was there, pumping Casey's lungs with an ambu bag and regarding her face, which she says seemed full of "recognition." You visit Casey's sister at the salon she works at called HAIRINDIPITY, then take her out to lunch. You eat French dips out of Styrofoam boxes, explain how she and Casey are "mouth twins," listen to a story about a poster she made for 4-H enumerating all the illnesses that affect farm goats. Later, you go down to the Bass Pro Shop and buy the gun Eli used, the same type of Chinese SKS, as well as the cheap off-brand folding stock, and you labor through the modifications. You become obsessed with a theory that there was a second shooter, then realize the same news sources promoting this idea also suggest that Eli worked for an Israeli death squad or was hypnotized by gun-control activists. "Dear Eli," you write, thinking you'll send him a letter. "As you can imagine," you say, but then feel so unnerved by those words that you step away from your computer. You look out your back window across Ozarka, but the shooting is all you can see or imagine. You want to follow the story long enough that it transforms into something else. But when you fall asleep, you dream of stepping on broken glass, that the gun in your closet is sentient and possessed with a desire to be used, and you wake up in the kitchen, the backyard, down a side street talking to an officer who thinks you're prowling. And when he gives you a ride home, you have to admit that all this is making you insane, though at this point in your life, sanity feels like such a shallow endeavor.

Then, on the night I'm called to give my testimony, I step onto the courtroom floor and I see you sitting alone in the back. Your legs are crossed. A legal pad rests on your knee. You're wearing a brightly dyed denim jacket. A headphone bud hangs from one ear, attached to a recording device. We have not talked in a meaningful way in some time, and when I see you from the stand, you don't look like a bereaved family member, someone who has been watching this surreal procession of testimonies for weeks. Instead, you look calm and engaged, like an avuncular journalist from out of town who is following the story.

So that night, I give you a long hug, say we're going out for a drink. "I will not accept no for an answer," I say, trying to make it sound like I need you, since I worry it is the opposite. All the local bars we frequent are far away, so we walk down to the Clarendon, a new boutique hotel that is the only high rise building in town. I picture it having one of those dark bars with wingback chairs and barrister bookshelves, but when we walk in, it's decorated like a tropical rainforest, with bamboo cabanas, string lights, and palm fronds suspended from the walls.

After sliding into a booth and ordering drinks, you look me in the eye, having waited for a quiet moment to speak your mind.

"I'm sorry," you say. "Being around you reminds me of the person I was back when Casey was alive."

Ever since the shooting, I've worried about this, because I was the main person you talked to about divorce, who probably spent too long validating your disappointment, when maybe all you needed was someone to throw your beer in the trash and tell you love is accepting someone for who they are. But I don't ask if this is what you mean. I'm afraid I might hurt you, not realizing how stupid that sounds.

"It's been a long time," I say.

You rearrange the menus on the table. "This trial is a sham. Every day I enter the courtroom, it feels like stepping off the street and into a theme park. My real life is out there, beyond the walls, getting farther and farther away."

"It does feel like that," I agree. "Just a bunch of people arguing about the velocity with which Eli's soul will arrive in hell. But then again, is there anything to gain from being a part of this process?"

You shake your head. "Nothing we do is going to bring them back."

When the waitress comes to refill our water glasses, we sit in silence.

She leaves.

"It's easy to feel far away when you keep being forced to look backward," I offer.

"It's easy to think you understand something after losing it," you respond, which seems like both an agreement and a rebuttal.

We drink a few more beers, talk about grading papers and your summer working on the farm, but it feels like a conversation we've scripted in advance.

Then you look over my shoulder, like something familiar is chewing its way out of the darkness.

"Professor Bishop!" someone says.

When I turn around, two people are walking toward us. One of them is Rose, her hair parted over the side of her face, wearing a pilled-out pea coat and black jeans. The other person is Scott, his fists jammed into the pockets of an ill-fitting jacket from an auto repair shop, curly hair shaved at its sides. They wave at us cautiously.

You invite them to sit down and introduce us, since we've never met, though we recognize each other from the courtroom. They order white Russians, and the sweet smell of Kahlua mixes with the dark beers we are drinking. There's no music, just soporific chatter from strangers in other booths rolling over us like warm, heavy rain.

Rose tells us about the birth revolution in Arkansas. She talks about being a student in your English class, and even recalls some of your lectures.

"Do you remember when you said there's nothing more romantic than dying for a lost cause?"

When she says this, it's clear it is meant to be a fun reminiscence. But for the past year, you've been taking every pithy theory you come across and jamming it into Eli's story to see how it fits. This one sounds like something you'd say if you wanted to encourage what he did.

"I was criticizing romanticism, right?" No one answers. You take a sip of your beer, then grimace. "God—did I really say that?"

She shrugs.

"Do you believe it?"

"I don't know."

"Good."

We laugh. You order another round. You ask Rose and Scott a lot of personal questions. How they met. How many siblings they have. Where they grew up. At first, I think it's because you're trying to steer the conversation far away from the trial. But when they leave for their hotel room upstairs, you smile and look around the room. Your face is partially colored by the blue tint of an aquarium, and it seems you've noticed something dense and all-encompassing in the atmosphere.

"That could be us," you say. "So easily."

When I ask what you mean, you start talking about Rose and Scott like the years and particulars that separate you are gone. It could be you: going to class, graduating, then making a family so you don't have to answer to the one you were given. Fighting off doubts about love and God by proclaiming your affection in conventional ways, then deciding real love should exonerate you from those proclamations. One day logging onto her computer only to find image searches for "hot young men with babies" and bookmarked articles titled 32 PHOTOS OF CELEBRITY DADS THAT WILL MAKE YOUR OVARIES WEEP. Then scrolling through those images, focusing on each infant, imagining yourself as a young father, and incorporating that image into your rehearsed future. It could be you, looking back on the beginning, regretting those times you waited angrily on the front porch when she was late, ultimately wondering what point nostalgia serves if it's for a past you wouldn't repeat even if given the chance.

At first, I'm not sure what you mean by all this. Later I understand you're opening up to me, telling the story of your life like it happened to someone else, like the things you've experienced are not singular, but part of a cycle that is always repeating and reinventing itself. And once I recognize this, we travel so far away from the moment that when we come back, I look past the lush unnatural vegetation and see, beyond the roving waiters and aquamarine fish tanks, an array of stars and clouds where the black ceiling used to be.

NO BEGINNING

ROSE

THERE ARE SOME DAYS, AFTER you and Scott get back from the trial, when the town that supposedly lost its ability to be normal appears to get it back. You walk to campus, past premature buds of dogwoods, swimming pools emptied of their dead leaves, into meadows of students marching through terraced lawns, faces shifting in the shadows of ironwood trees. By now, all the memorial gardens have been dedicated, the leftover donations re-gifted, and if anyone mentions the shooting, they say something like, "I'm glad Eli's story has finally come to an end," as if they just watched the mediocre finale of a once-beloved sitcom. In class, topics like biological essentialism no longer seem imbued with newer, darker meanings. You study reproductive systems, memorize skeletal muscles. Afterward, you meet up with Deborah, who walks you through hypnobirthing scripts that ask you to focus on a knitted argyle uterus, imagine its cervix yielding to intrauterine pressure. When she does this, the room dematerializes. There is no patterned curtain encircling the door, no raised blinds, no cars multiplying on the highway, just a fetus descending through the fabric.

Later, you describe all this to Scott, who shows up at your apartment holding your vibrator, a bottle of wine, and cherry-flavored lube he got at a safe sex symposium. You tell him the whole day feels softened by the tint of a dream, and that's when he pulls a book from his jacket and reads you a poem. It's a cloying sonnet about boundless love, filled with words like "whilst" and "eternity," but when he finishes reading, he says the point is not that he feels this way about you now, but that he can imagine doing so in the future.

But then there are days when Eli's sentence feels like the beginning, not the end. After all, you've spent your entire adult life learning that the dead return—it's what they do. On these days, a dirty moon hangs in the afternoon sky and the dogwoods are already falling around you like pink snow. News breaks that several bereaved families are filing civil suits against the university, and once again, people are writing op-eds explaining how real Christian forgiveness must cost the transgressor something. Students are interrupting class to ask, "Why is no one held accountable anymore?" When you leave campus, you try to take solace in your doula work, but your new client is yet another gender-conforming middle-class white woman obsessed with natural products, natural labors, and natural parenting. She tries to impress you with facts about the medical industrial complex, and it makes the whole "being brave for others" idea seem like just an exclusionary sham. At night, you drive to Scott's house, watch half of a murkily pretentious horror film, then go to bed, but Scott keeps waking up from nightmares. A stranger touching his neck, admitting she doesn't know how to feel for a pulse. A janitor mopping blood in a corner, refusing to turn and face him. When he sits up in bed, you walk him through how to visit all the muscles in his body. You say he is an old coat thrown across a chair. Soon it is quiet, except for the frog noises from the marsh outside, the old furnace clicking on and dimming the lights. Now it's you who can't sleep, because some horrible possibility is beneath the surface of everything. You go outside for a smoke under stars that look like one light shining through a wall of porous rock, and you wonder if the scariest thing about all this is not that life can't return to normal, but that it already has.

Spring approaches summer like this, with each day mutating between two realities, until Scott graduates and gets an email from a quasi-famous artist in Seattle. The guy's name is Jal Peck, and he's known for sculpting heroic male statues then pushing them over at his exhibits, at which point he invites guests to stand on their plinths like they've overthrown a despot. He tells Scott to consider applying for the graduate program where he teaches. "You understand that there is no heart in a sculpture, only chaos," he writes. When Scott recites this, you're able to share some of his excitement, but you're also off balance. You have two years left at OU, and already college is starting to seem like a place that conceals one truth for each one it exposes. You keep this thought to yourself until the next day, when you're driving to Wal-Mart and listening to the Abortion Diary Podcast, which you discover was founded by two women your age who met at the Jane Paltrow Center for Allied Birth, also in Seattle.

Later on in life, you'll recognize how this moment is barely even a coincidence, but right now it feels like a sign. You call Scott to say you want to move to Seattle with him. And what surprises both of you is not how hasty the decision is, or how intangible your imaginings, but how little you need to justify leaving.

So you save your money. You sell your belongings. You call a myriad of landlords, most of whom rent "efficiency units" that are long bus rides from the inner city, zoned for hot plates and shared bathrooms. You attend going-away parties where your friends infiltrate local bars, throw cake in your face, tell you in the orange tint of bar lights about that one time they moved to Austin or LA or New York. How their Craigslist roommate cured meat in the hall closet and argued with debt collectors at 5 a.m. How their shitty jobs and dwindling bank accounts eventually brought them back home. You drink too much, wake up hungover when you're supposed to meet your parents. They cry as they drive you to the airport, where you wait in a lobby decorated with taxidermy and a water wheel. And when it's time to go, you board a small feeder flight straight from the hot tarmac.

Most of the seats are empty, the plastic armrests discolored with age. You bite your nails, watch the sunlight glow through the oval windows, smell sweat mixing with reheated turkey sandwiches. And when you take off, summiting the molting clouds that spread over the interior highlands, you think about your friends' stories about leaving, then coming back. You find it reassuring the mistakes they made underestimated homesickness, the indifference of strangers, or the size of a budget. You're glad those are the reasons they returned, and not because what they found was simply another home, brutal in the exact same way. You don't want the only notch against Ozarka to be that it's where you're coming from, and not where you're going.

Every morning, you wake up in Seattle without a plan. Fog rolls through the city like smoke from a forest fire. Your apartment is cluttered with furniture from bourgeois free piles. Your fridge is filled with leftover pastries, pear gorgonzola pizza, and Vietnamese noodle soup. You don't shower, just step out onto the sidewalk, catch an accordion bus that gasps around every corner. You feel like you have entered a second life whose beginning you have yet to find. You have no job, school, or social obligations. All you have is Scott and enough money to be unemployed for several months.

Somehow, none of this is scary. Nowadays, you accept that you have no godlike ability to weigh one life against another. You get day-drunk at art museums, take photographs at strange rocky beaches, breathe in the smell of brine and Douglas fir. You make acquaintances with people who take you to electropop concerts in the back of vintage jewelry stores, who bring you to design firms filled with jagged ferns and people wearing complicated scarves. You sit with them in quiet meadows of urban parks, where everyone is smoking weed and throwing Frisbees as well-groomed dogs run laps around dahlia gardens and retaining ponds. These people ask if you like it here, and when you say yes, they sigh a little. They say the real city died five years ago, when such-and-such dive bar/music venue/teriyaki shop was priced out by the tech boom and turned into condos. What they don't realize is that, to you, Seattle is just a city. What matters is that it's different, not that it's authentic.

Eventually you run out of money. A friend gets you a job at a French bistro down by the public market, which you feel less proud about once you realize all the waitresses are also dark-complexioned brunettes with strong jaw lines. They put you on the breakfast shift, and you work alone as customers filter in from the blurry weather. Business is slow, but tips are good, and when the manager fazes you at lunchtime, you drink aperitif wine at the bar, then spend the afternoon wandering the city. You talk to street canvassers about reproductive health. You read irreverent newspapers in urban parks. You buy street food and wander past all the giant cranes and primary-colored condos you have yet to develop distaste for. These days, you feel like you're losing responsibilities instead of gaining them, like time is moving back toward innocence instead of away from it.

Then one day, you're running entrees from the kitchen when you see a homeless-looking man waiting by the hostess stand. He's wearing a dirty army surplus jacket, a drab blanket draped around his shoulders, and he smells like a goat barn. As you approach him, you decide it's not your job to interrogate potential customers. "Table for one?" you say, and he says, "Sure." You lead him to a seat by the window, give him a menu, and when you come back with water, he orders broiled eggs and an escarole salad. He eats quietly, scanning the dining room like someone looking over the top of his eyeglasses, though he isn't wearing any. When he's done, you drop off the bill, and that's when he takes a deep breath and lets out an insulted sigh.

"Way too much," he says.

You pause, realizing you can hear the radio in the kitchen, which is usually buried under all the noise of customers talking and eating.

"I'm sorry," you say, "but those are the prices."

The man dumps a few crumpled bills and change on the table. "This is all I have."

You grab each bill and flatten it out in your hand, then place it in the check holder. "It's fine this time," you say, "but you can't come back." Then, instead of waiting for a response, you walk to the back of the restaurant, where your view is obscured by the espresso machine, and you wait for him to leave.

When he does, you decide you're satisfied with how you handled the situation. But then you're at the register, calculating how much to take from your tips to pay the difference, when another customer approaches you. He stands with his foot beyond the threshold that separates the kitchen from the dining area. Before he says anything, he smiles. It's the self-satisfied smile of a man who is proud of an idea, like it's a present he's about to give himself.

"Sure are a lot of psychos in this city," he says.

"I guess so."

"They'll keep taking advantage of girls like you, if you don't watch out."

"Okay," you mumble. You try to appear busy by poking at the register. You ring in eight entrees for no one.

"Anyway," he says, "I want you to have this."

He grabs your hand and drops something into it. When you look down, you realize you're holding a pocketknife. It's a beautiful piece with a rosewood handle, edges fastened by silver bolsters.

"Just in case," he says, already pedaling backwards, like he just said you're pretty and is pretending to want nothing in return.

For the rest of the day, the knife nags at you with all that it implies. You keep it in your apron pocket, which means when you reach for a pen or a wine key, you sometimes accidentally clasp its heavy frame like an iron bar. When this happens, you see yourself as that customer must have seen you, as some naïve girl whose biggest fear is a poor person emerging from a badly lit street. You picture yourself shuffling between tables on the old porcelain tile with your pink lipstick, your lace blouse buttoned up to the neck, nodding like a demure student when Francophiles correct your pronunciation. It makes you wonder if this is what you get for wishing, deep down, to be seen as someone who has survived nothing. Maybe "girls like you" is part of the carapace of privilege you're trying to hide beneath, and you can't be upset when people treat you accordingly.

You try to let go of this thought, but it's one of those feelings that, once named, is evident everywhere—like the knife is being handed to you over and over again. You're eating waffles at a brunch party when you realize everyone is talking about the housing crisis with academic detachment. You're putting on makeup in the bathroom when a coworker says, "Your eyes are so *exotic* for a white girl." You're telling people you're from Arkansas, then listening to them sneer at the idea of it, like it's some separate racist society they don't belong to. Or you're talking to a friend who says he was inspired to teach at a low-income/high-minority high school after watching a TV show about teenage drug dealers in West Baltimore. "I don't believe in power," he says later, in the party room of a condo, one with black and white prints of Kurt Cobain mounted on the walls. "All power is just inferiority, anyway."

What bothers you most about these moments is not that they upset your cultural sensibilities, but that, somewhere along the way, you lost the authority to explain why. After all these years of trying to look like a private-educated white ex-suburbanite, people are finally mistaking you for one, and instead of feeling accepted, you feel like an imposter. You start mourning that awkward preteen girl who wandered grassy sidewalks while her mom donated plasma, who slept on yoga mats with her brother in the aftermath of hot sunsets. You wonder when you started to mistake success for a status-mongering erasure of the person you once were. You decide to carry that girl with you into the future, but you're not sure where she is anymore, or how to get her back.

Amidst all this, you and Scott are invited to a show at a party bar down by the shipping wharf. The band you're there to see is called Mommy Issues, an industrial synthpunk trio whose lead singer is known for stretching his shirt over his face and shouting through the fabric. When they start playing, a giant man with a villainous forehead starts pushing everyone near the stage. Several other large men join him, and a stray elbow rips across your ear. You can't see, and you lose Scott, so you retreat to the back of the venue, where the smell of old beer mixes with urinal cakes. You stand there for another song, but you can only hear the tinny ring of cymbals and a synthesizer like agitated violins, so you give up and head out to the smoking patio, where you lean against a wood planter cradling a dead bush.

You wait for several minutes, then check your phone out of boredom, discovering someone commented on a photo you posted of an old train station. "Seattle looks cool," they say. "How's it going?" You realize it's Johnny. This is the first time he's contacted you since that Delta Nu party, and his casual tone is maddening. You always imagined he felt guilty and conflicted about what happened. But now, it's clear you've been giving him the benefit of the doubt.

Eventually, Scott comes outside looking for you.

"What are you doing out here?" he asks, still catching his breath, steam dancing off his shoulders.

"I'm not a fan of the whole mosh pit thing."

"Never been to a punk show before?" He laughs, but you don't laugh with him, because it feels like condescension masquerading as humor.

"Looked to me like a bunch of men pushing people around like they always do," you say, with an extra edge of irritation.

For some reason, this makes Scott furious. He starts explaining how punk music has always been egalitarian, which you listen to passively, staring down the alley toward a row of houseboats lining the dark rim of the shore. When he realizes your disinterest, he swallows the rest of his beer, shakes the empty can, then walks back into the venue. You wait there, thinking about how you always hold yourself responsible for the emotions of your male counterparts, how you adopt their grievances as your own, and often blame yourself for them. You think: why does this never work the other way around? Then, instead of going back inside, you exit through a back door into the empty street, where a patch of highway roars from beyond a cement divider. You start walking, unsure of where you are until you find the downtown skyline, which is dominated by new oblong skyscrapers hovering over the old symmetrical ones. They are lit dramatically with the colors of local sports teams, pointing to the sky like futuristic cathedrals.

You walk for three miles, past empty buses, shadowy department stores, and restaurant workers rolling garbage bins to the curb. You worry where Scott is, then get mad at yourself for worrying. You write him a long text explaining how people with no misogynist animosity in their hearts can still uphold misogynist institutions. You walk in circles, editing it for grammar and punctuation, then realize how meaningless this point is when held up against your sadness, which is all-encompassing. So you delete it, try to call Abby and Henry, then Ellen and Deborah, but no one answers. You can't walk back to your apartment because if Scott is there, your relationship may not survive whatever argument will ensue, and if he's not there, you'll have to sit and worry until he returns. So you keep wandering the streets alone. You're trapped inside your life. You hear that drumbeat of coalescing impulses—one that will use anything it can to bargain with fear.

So you walk into the first hotel you see, one that looks old and cheap from the outside, but inside is all baroque architecture, contemporary jazz, and mantels with complicated bouquets. You look more out of place than expected as you talk to the concierge with your puffy eyes, no coat or bags, wearing a doll collar dress. You get a room for $300, which you put on your credit card, then run to it like you're being chased. Inside, you raid the wet bar, start drinking whisky from a coffee mug, then switch to vodka. You open the French doors that lead to a Juliet balcony with a view of the Space Needle. You turn on the television, flip past cartoons, action movies, *The People's Court*, end up on a documentary about the mortal dangers of escalators. You're looking for something that registers or affects you, but nothing does. All the noise, the strata of buildings beyond the window, the matronly floral patterns on the drapes—it's all part of a disconnected landscape your vast inner life has already spread across. With no distractions left, you spiral down. You admit that you left your job, your family, and dropped out of college to run toward a false horizon. You've been here six months and all you've done is try to desert your former life, only to realize it has already deserted you.

The transition from panic to resolution happens quickly. Suddenly, you get the idea that there is a nothingness out there that will accept you and make you into itself. When this happens, you go to the extra-deep soaking tub in the bathroom, one that sits on a platform with a territorial view of the city. You fill it with hot water. You get in. Now that you're ready, it feels good, like you've entered a place where no memory can harm you. You stare out the window for a long time, into the ceiling of clouds illuminated by light pollution, realizing you haven't seen the stars since you came here. You've been living in the absence of the universe.

Eventually, you reach for your purse, spilling lukewarm water all over the floor. You dig through it until you find the knife the customer gave to you. You peel the blade from its handle, tilt it into the light, trying to limn out your reflection in the metal. Here, you recall one of the few thin memories you have of your father. In this memory, he is sitting at the yellow Formica table in the kitchen with his brother. He says one night, just after he married your mother, a man came up the road and asked for help because his car broke down. But when your father stepped out and asked where the car was, the man said, "Keep walking, and you'll find it," which your father repeats like it's a punch line. He sips his beer, looks away, and the story ends. For a long time, you thought this was a joke, or a dream. Later, you wondered if some man abducted your mother, and this was your father's way to tell you. But now, it's starting to blend with other stories men have told you over the years. They use different words, but their intent is always the same: to keep you in awe of violence and the power that it supposedly holds over you.

You don't know why you end up losing your nerve. You don't feel any resolve, or grace, or anything beyond panic and resignation. So you drain the tub, dry off, hunch over the mini bar, and eat almost the entire array of chocolates and snacks that will be billed to you later at exorbitant prices. And when you're done, you crouch on the floor beside the bed, your hotel-issued bathrobe spreading out around you like a giant mop, and you fall asleep while eleven voicemails accumulate on your phone.

You wake up the next morning to a balcony spewing sudden daylight. It's still January, but the whole city is swollen with blue. The tops of tall buildings glitter. You open the door and lean over the railing, watch pedestrians crowd around buskers on street corners, cyclists bottlenecking at traffic lights, seagulls lounging in water sculptures. You look into the deep shadows of forked channels, the ocean water laminated with sun, the snow-veined mountains sharpening against the sky. You do this for a long time, savoring how clean and empty you feel. You are thankful to be back in the world, to be once again part of its imagery.

This is when you turn on your phone and call Scott. For a moment, you worry about being scolded for running away, but then you decide not to feel guilty, because so much in your life has depended on your obedience to shame. So when he answers, you just ask how he's doing. "I'm so sorry," he says, his voice soft and unfamiliar. "Where are you?"

At this point, you laugh, because you don't even know the name of the hotel you're in. You describe it to him the best you can, telling him about the balcony, the heap of preposterous throw pillows on your bed, the smell of tortilla chips from a Tacos Guaymas across the street. You end up talking for a long time, like old friends hoping to fill in the years that separate them. At one point, Scott tells you he's been researching chainsaw art, sends you a few sketches of wooden bears. One is standing on a stump, holding a placard that says KILL ALL YUPPIES, while another kneels on the ground, arms tied behind his back like a fettered prisoner. "I love it," you say. "I love how you are always taking two very different things and insisting they belong together." It is a statement that ends up meaning more than you intend. It seems to explain why you matter so much to each other, why the hurt and brokenness of one day does not carry into another the way it used to.

This is the last time, at least for many years, that you consider leaving. You stay in Seattle, chasing days of uninterrupted happiness, which come more often than they ever have before. You go back to school, work for a nonprofit that connects low-resource families with volunteer doulas. Scott builds custom tree houses, transfers to home restoration, decides against grad school entirely. Together, you take ferry rides to small islands, sing "Dirt Road Anthem" and "Amarillo Sky" at karaoke nights hosted by drag queens. You move into a basement apartment that feels like the damp hull of a ship, though its back door opens to a patio sheltered by the long wing of a bigleaf maple. Your life is good, but there are, of course, times when you and Scott desert each other, when your love calcifies into a thin friendship, when you're not sure who you are alone. You're standing in your neglected garden, watching the fat window of the sky darken with a storm. You're carrying your shoes up the basement stairs, your body like a shadow hanging from a rope. During these times, your life is not your own, but some dream you inherited, one that is so close to ending you might as well bring it all the way. You stare at that rosewood knife, which you now display on a bookshelf, where it's supposed to be a reminder of a feeling you escaped. But have you?

You hold the knife in your hand, then put it back, remembering how foolish you are for trying to understand something by destroying it. You take a shower, try to clear your head. You go down to your local Laundromat—the dingy one painted like a toy castle, with stolen shopping carts scattered in front like capsized boats—so you can feel productive. You end up watching the news on a muted television mounted to the ceiling, and a familiar face appears. It's a young man leaning against a washed-out brick wall, lips curling inward, eyes drifting away from the camera with a slight attitude of mystery. You know him, but he's from an untraceable era of your life. You wonder what classmate, what cousin, what old coworker this is, until the scene changes to a prison compound, and you realize it's Eli.

At first, this disturbs you. Your memories are hopelessly scrambled. You're too convinced of the absence of monsters. But then, you think maybe it's fine Eli has collapsed into a weak point of light over your shoulder. Maybe he shouldn't be allowed to stand beside an event like that and take credit for what happened. After all, no one has had the luxury of starting from the beginning—not even you.

TO ALL WHOM THESE PRESENTS SHALL COME

EDDIE

TO ALL WHOM THESE PRESENTS SHALL COME is the salutation the governor writes on Eli's death warrant, before fixing the time and date of his execution. It has been twelve years, but the state has finally secured a dose of potassium chloride, reportedly donated by an anonymous supplier in the prison's parking lot. What this means is that, for the third time this year, you are driving to Feliciana with your phone mounted on the dash, waiting for a clemency hearing update. You are imagining the worst outcome of this event—Eli's body thrashing off a table, his father clawing at the door—hoping that to foresee an elaborate detail will prevent it from happening.

But this time, it's different. The darkness on I-40 is barely cut by moonlight. Your phone does not light up. By the time you are alone in the woods, some adrenaline has worn off. You are a horse continuing to run long after its rider has fallen into the dirt. You think: this is what real endings feel like, after anxiety erodes into routine.

When you arrive at Feliciana, Eli has already been in a bright room for thirty hours with a Bible and a chaplain. A major has collected his belongings. He has bowed under a wood sign that says SILENCE, his leg irons rattling across the floor. After being strapped into a gurney, a nurse has evaluated his veins, then hooked him to intravenous tubes that feed through a small hole in the wall. While sitting through fifteen minutes of pre-drug saline solution, he has watched a teal curtain out of the corner of his eyes, waiting for it to open onto the viewing room. He has been assured that the midazolam will anesthetize him completely.

Meanwhile, you are escorted to a small brick room, where you sit in a row of chairs with Eli's father, the warden, the chaplain, and five volunteer witnesses. When the curtain opens, you're surprised by how Eli's gurney is shaped like a surfboard and mounted on a thin pedestal, giving it the effect of hovering in the air. Never in your life have you seen a body presented this way, like it has been installed somewhere for observation.

After a few minutes, the warden approaches the window and touches his eyeglasses, like a coach feeding his team an important signal.

"Do you have any last words?" he says, arms crossed, face emptied of all expression.

"Yes, sir, I do," says Eli. He does not turn his head to the side. He is positioned in such a way that the most natural place to look is toward the ceiling.

"I want to say that I am sorry for any pain that I have caused," he says. "I didn't understand what I was doing. Something was missing, and the shooting was my way of trying to get it back."

Over the last year, you have exchanged several short letters with Eli, which means you're used to these types of phrases. You no longer focus on the passive voice, the boilerplate lack of responsibility. Nowadays, you are trying to see your own place in all of this. You are considering that, if indeed there was a voice, maybe you have heard it, too.

When Eli is done speaking, you have to close your eyes. You thought you'd be able to watch, but you've lost sight of why you came here. You thought this could be a way of extending compassion toward him, but now you can't imagine how compassion could possibly work this way.

When you open your eyes, Eli's skin has turned slightly crimson, but his body is in the same position. Everyone stands, and when they crowd around a folding table to sign paperwork, you do not feel as if anything has come to an end. It's just that another thread running through your life has prematurely vanished.

Back in the prison parking lot, the sun is coming up beyond the fangsome treeline, its peachy residue infecting the corners of the sky. You get in your car, but you don't leave. You watch the protesters and SWAT team disperse, wondering why this story, and all the ones like it, have to end this way.

So you start your car and drive home, woozy with images of concertina wire, gun towers, the intaglio of trees and swamps. You try to understand what just happened, to see how it might fit into the always-shifting geometry of your past. But then you stop. You remind yourself it's okay to be confused, that you can't flick the lights on quick enough to see what the darkness looks like.

When you emerge from the forest and onto a stretch of familiar highway, you decide you shouldn't be alone. I'll be in class by the time you get back to Ozarka. So you cycle through a list of friends to call, struck by an increasingly familiar realization that you're not very close to anyone. The people you know are compassionate and giving, but you'd need hours to catch them up on your life in general, not to mention the entangled notions of compassion and shame that took you to Feliciana and back.

You're about to pass through Little Rock. You consider stopping at your parents' house, but driving through the quiet streets of Marin Estates has always felt wrong. Whenever you go home, you still wish you were taking a left on Alameda, toward that brick house you lived in before high school, the one with the back deck surrounded by unkempt boxwood. You want to enter the house and then wander outside, the porch light thickening around you. You want your mother to emerge from the back room and massage your

shoulders until the entire house shakes from the garage door opening. You want to run downstairs so you can watch your father pull
his Buick into a space just wide enough for it to fit. You want him
to do something silly, like keep his sunglasses on, or put his tie in
his mouth as he parks, to indicate he had a good day. And before
he cuts the engine, you want to sing part of a song you learned in
choir, emboldened by his good mood. You want to feel no risk when
expressing your joy, your doubt, or your frailty.

For most of your adult life, you assumed that longing for this
place was just nostalgia, an ordinary regret of growing older. But
after you get back to Ozarka and sit alone on my porch, you start
to think it's evidence of a rift. "Something was missing," you hear
Eli say again. The phrase unspools like a stray dream. It no longer
sounds like an empty grab at sympathy. Instead, it suggests an era of
comfort and connection, before the people he loved turned into long
corridors he was told not to enter. It makes you wonder if, all this
time, maybe you and Eli were missing the same thing. Maybe you're
different from each other only in degree, not in kind.

Later, when I get home, you explain all this to me. You take
me back to that house on Alameda, that garage where you sang "O
Magnum Mysterium" beneath the hum of an engine, surrounded by
camping gear, inherited furniture, and bins of old clothing. You tell
me that, at some point, you traded in this person for someone else.
You were trying to grow up. You thought you were getting stronger
and more independent. You were setting yourself apart as a man. But
it didn't work the way you thought. You expressed your emotions so
infrequently that Casey often felt blindsided by them. You went on
some inner journey after her death because you assumed your grief
would be displeasing to others. And as the years passed, you got farther away from everyone, because you weren't growing up. You were
taking what had bloomed and folding it back upon itself. You were
dying on the inside. And what you are beginning to understand is

that, when this type of rotten limb finally does break apart, we don't examine its decay. All we ever focus on is the sound, as clean and sudden as a gunshot.

ACKNOWLEDGMENTS

I AM INCREDIBLY GRATEFUL to everyone who helped write this book. To my close friends and trusted readers: Caroline Beimford, who edited the first pages I wrote, back when the last chapter was the first; Kaj Tanaka, who told me to trust my instincts; Corina Zappia, who discussed point of view over late-night pie; and Diana Xin, who told me to slow down. Thanks to Rilla Askew and Molly Giles for the many forms your mentorship has taken. To my parents Sheila, John, Amy, Mike, and my sister Natasha for your unqualified love and support. Thanks to Christine Texeira and Hugo House for inviting this project into your community. To the other Hugo House fellows: Sierra Golden, Sarah Kate Moore, Quenton Baker, and Kathy Harding. To all my friends in Fayetteville for those formative years. To Alex and Caitie for the coffee and conversation. Thanks to *Moss* and *Vol. 1 Brooklyn* for publishing excerpts. To Padma Viswanathan and Rebecca Brown for your early endorsements. To Chelsea Werner-Jatzke, Matt Muth, Josh Fomon, Katie Lee Ellison, and Richard Chiem for your camaraderie. To Diante, who read an early draft and talked to me about writing mid-shift at the grill station. Thanks to everyone at Dzanc, especially Michelle Dotter, for your editorial insight, tenacity, and for giving this book a home. And to Katharine Toombs, who gave everything: inspiration, edits, a love that challenges, and a year of solitude at the tanker desk we carried up that flight of twisted stairs.